Block City

Pam Greer

Published by Lechner Syndications

www.lechnersyndications.com

ISBN 13: 978-1-927794-20-3

"When legs can't play anymore, play with your heart."

~Anonymous

.

CONTENTS

CHAPTER 1

This was crazy exciting!

As Neeka Leigh pulled her overnight bag from the back of her ma's SUV, the early morning sun beating against her back, she couldn't help but savor how epic today was for the Hickory Academy volleyball program. Both JV and varsity were heading to Jackson University to attend an elite volleyball camp, one they hoped would give their team the advantage they needed to get to State. The previous two seasons, Hickory Academy had come so close to realizing their goals, winning their District and Regional tournaments, only to lose at Sub-State. Neeka wouldn't let all they'd achieved go to waste. She would make sure they got a chance to battle it out at the State tournament this year. She had a plan, and the volleyball camp at Jackson University was the first step.

She hugged Little Joe, an inflatable cactus with big red sunglasses and a cowboy hat, which she was holding in her arms.

"Found it!" declared Payton Moore, Neeka's best friend, holding her MP3 player above her thick brown hair as she jumped out of the backseat of the SUV. Her light green eyes were shining against her pale skin. She was as excited about Jackson University as Neeka was. They all were.

"Let me guess, it was under the seat, just like I said, and not in your equipment bag," Neeka deduced, already knowing the answer.

Payton ignored her but continued to smile as she pulled her bags out of the back.

Lawanda Leigh, Neeka's ma, double-checked the SUV, making sure everything they needed was unloaded. "Your first trip away from home. With your brother off at college out of state and your dad leaving for work about the time I get home, the house will feel empty with both my kids gone."

"You've had the house to yourself before, Ma," Neeka reminded her. "Every time we go to Memaw's during the summer."

Lawanda sighed and kissed Neeka on the forehead. "Yeah, but this time feels different. More permanent. You're sixteen years old. Soon, you'll be going off to college as well, and not just for the few nights you're at volleyball camp. Forever."

"If I'm in college forever, you'd better start saving up."

Her ma wasn't usually so weepy, quite the opposite actually, but she knew it was an emotional week. They'd said goodbye to Jamari, her brother, only a few days before. He'd left early to help out with his school's orientations. He was on an academic scholarship, but he needed the summer job to help him buy his books for the semester. Neeka couldn't believe books could cost in the hundreds!

Neeka hugged her ma. "I bet you and Papa break out a bottle of champagne the night I leave for college."

Her ma's serious expression didn't waiver. "I'll see you at the end of the week. Stay out of trouble. I took the liberty of removing those super soakers from your bag."

Payton scrunched up her nose in disappointment, but Neeka thought it was for the best. They needed to concentrate at camp if they wanted to get to State. If their Sub-State match against Cumberland Lake High School last year had taught them anything, it was that they had a long way to go with their skills if they wanted to play at the top level.

Payton suddenly groaned. "I forgot my sunscreen! I left it in your room near your telescope. I took it out of my bag last night when I was putting on my pajamas."

"Don't worry, I have lots," Neeka reassured her. Her skin was dark brown, like the short spirals of her hair, but it still freckled under the sun. Neeka hated her freckles. They were cute on some girls, but not her. She always carried around a lot of sunscreen.

Her ma said her last goodbyes and left the girls alone in the parking lot to join their team.

"*We're going to Jackson!*" Payton began singing as she picked her bags up off the curb. "*Hotter than a pepper sprout!*"

"Do you even know what a pepper sprout is?"

"Nope."

Neeka paused beside Payton, watching as the rest of their teammates grouped together near the gym doors. It was amazing what a difference a few months could make. A lot of the girls had grown, like Selina Cho and Courtney Adams. In fact, it was quite possible Courtney was as tall as Payton, if not taller. Neeka had grown as well, but she was still one of the shortest on the team, so she didn't think anyone would notice.

Besides their height, many of the girls had changed their personal appearance. Selina had cut her already short hair into a super tiny pixie cut. But the heavy rock chic make-up she used to accentuate her Asian features remained the same. Valerie Sutton's auburn hair was as shiny as ever, but she had put purple streaks into it, a bold move for the beauty queen. The most dramatic change was Janette Daiser's. Instead of her usual mousy brown hair, Janette had dyed it a light golden blonde color and let it grow out, long and wavy.

"God, I haven't seen most of these girls since the fundraiser last year," Payton revealed. "I've been so busy, I lost touch with most of them."

"Me too," Neeka admitted. "Even Selina. The last time I saw her was the end-of-the-year BBQ she threw at her house in June, right before her family left to go traveling around Europe. I had no idea she'd cut her hair so short."

"Maybe it's a European thing. It looks great, though."

Neeka watched as her teammates hugged and laughed, catching up after being apart for so many weeks. "We've all changed so much." She turned, looking Payton over. "Except you. You're the same ole Payton I've always known—eating, sleeping, and breathing sports."

Payton laughed. "I hope that's not an insult! But I have changed. I don't feel as insecure as I used to be. Volleyball has taught me that I don't have to be perfect at everything, that I'm still a leader and liked, even if my best friend outshines me." She jabbed Neeka playfully.

"Yeah, well, don't let Selina hear you say that. Now that Coach Mike has told her she'll start for varsity this year, I reckon she's taken her eyes off you and now sees me as her biggest competition."

"I'd be lying if I didn't say that was a relief," Payton said. "But she's a hitter; you're a setter. What could she possibly be competing with you for?"

"The admiration of the coaches."

Payton nodded knowingly. "Selina is a decent friend off the court, but she is a total machine on the court. She sees everyone as competition."

Walking toward the group from the van she had just parked nearby, Coach Gina Williams, the assistant coach, noticed Neeka and Payton standing near the curb and enthusiastically waved them over, nearly knocking her signature designer sunglasses off her short, curly black hair as she did. Dressed in a chiffon blouse and white shorts that set off her tan legs, she looked as if she was heading to a fashion show in New York, not a high school volleyball camp.

"Here we go," Neeka said. "Our third season. They always say third time lucky."

"No," Payton said, shaking her head. "Not lucky. We work hard. That's how we've gotten so far in such a short time, and it's why this year, we will make it to State."

Jackson was nearly a three-hour drive away, including the numerous breaks the coaches predicted the girls would need to use the bathroom and stretch their legs. With almost twenty girls, from freshmen to seniors, shoved into two vans, the coaches honked as they departed the Hickory Academy parking lot.

"And we're off!" Coach Gina chirped.

A half hour in, Neeka found herself squished between Courtney and Payton, who was sound asleep on her shoulder.

"Payton! You're drooling all over me. What are you, a Saint Bernard?"

"What?" Payton asked, only halfway waking up, her head dipping forward.

Neeka removed the hoodie she was wearing, the shoulder of which was now covered in drool, and bunching it up into a pillow, put it against

4

the window opposite her and gently set Payton's head against it.

"Girl sure is a slobbering mess," Courtney remarked.

"You're one to talk. If another one of your cornrows hits me in the eye, I'm going to cut them off. What do you have at the end of those things, rocks?"

"They're beads made out of jade. I thought it would be a good color—a mix of blue and green, Hickory Academy's colors."

"Well, maybe you should keep your school spirit to something that won't give me a black eye."

"It's not my fault we're squished like sardines in the back of this van," Courtney huffed.

In the front, Coach Gina drove while two seniors listened to music beside her. Like Payton, Janette and Selina were sound asleep in the middle row of seats. Val, sitting on the outside next to Selina, sent text messages from her phone, likely to Stephen, her boyfriend. A second van driven by Coach Michael Ross, the head coach of Hickory Academy's volleyball program, followed behind them.

Upon hearing Courtney complain, Val turned around in her seat. "Leave Courtney alone. Her beads look great. She could be the next Zendaya, that Disney actress."

It was true. With her model looks, Courtney looked good in anything, even a head full of jade. She could easily pass for a young Hollywood starlet.

"You could be the next Zendaya too," Courtney said to Neeka. "Especially now that you're a bit taller."

They both knew that wasn't true. Neeka was pretty in a classic way, but she wasn't stunning, not like Courtney. But she was delighted Courtney had noticed that she had grown, even if it was only by a couple of inches. She had hoped someone would.

"Have you seen the new *Hunger Games* movie?" Neeka asked, thinking the two and a half hours they still had to drive would be a good time to get to know the girls better. She didn't really talk to Val and Courtney outside of volleyball. They were hard girls to get to know. Val was Miss Popular among the lowerclassmen, but beneath her peppy smile was a girl with a very high guard up. Courtney had only transferred to Hickory

Academy last year from California, and in that time, the only person she'd really gotten close to was Val.

"I thought it was excellent!" Courtney shrieked. "Peeta is super cute."

Val agreed with her. "I was so excited when they kissed for the first time."

"I actually thought it was all a bit silly," Neeka confessed. "I mean, they're out fighting for their lives. Who cares about romance?"

"Everyone," Courtney pointed out. "Why do you think the movie is such a hit?"

"Still..." Neeka shrugged her shoulders. "I just don't think he would fall in love with her that quickly."

Val looked as if Neeka's words saddened her. "Do you not believe in love from afar?" she asked.

"No," Neeka said truthfully. "I believe you can like someone from afar, but love is a whole other story. Why? Did you love Stephen from afar?"

Stephen was a lacrosse player. Val had been dating him since last winter. They seemed really happy together and were probably one of the stronger couples at Hickory Academy.

"I guess not," Val said. "But we're in love now. He told me he loved me right before I left for camp."

"OMG!" Courtney exclaimed loudly, causing the sleeping girls to stir.

"Selina for MVP," Selina muttered, falling back to sleep.

Lowering her voice, Courtney murmured, "Why didn't you tell me?"

"It only just happened when he picked me up this morning. My mom had to work, so he insisted on driving me down. I haven't had time to tell anyone. I'm still processing it."

"Well, I'm happy you're happy," Neeka said sincerely.

"Do you like anyone?" Courtney asked her.

Neeka tried to keep a neutral expression. She did have a crush on someone, but she didn't want anyone to know. It was a secret not even Payton knew. The boy liked someone else, of this she was certain, so there was no point bringing it up.

"No one worth mentioning," she said. "What about you, Courtney?"

Courtney rolled her eyes. "Please. These Southern boys are nothing like the boys in California."

"You're right, they're better," Val quipped. She raised her hand to high-five Neeka.

"I thought your parents were from Nashville?" Neeka asked after slapping Val's hand. "Isn't that why you guys moved back here, to be closer to family?"

"Yeah," Courtney confirmed. "My auntie only lives like ten minutes from the school. She's great. She's my dad's youngest sister, so she's not much older than we are. She graduated from college last year, and now she has her own place. Her apartment is amazing. Val's been there. It's really chic and modern, like something out of the magazines. Actually, I think Payton's mom was her interior designer."

This surprised Neeka. Payton never mentioned anything about her mom working for Courtney's auntie. But then again, Payton probably didn't know herself. She and her mom were complete opposites. Payton loved sports and hot dogs. Allison Moore loved fabrics and beauty salons. The two got along, but there was a natural divide between them.

Val suddenly remembered something. "We need to get a photo of Little Joe on the journey to camp!"

"Selina already did," Neeka told her. "She put him in the driver's seat of the van and positioned his arms to look as if he was beeping the horn."

Little Joe was a mini version of Big Joe, the gigantic inflatable cactus in their school's cafeteria. The girls had thrown a fundraiser last year to pay for their camp fees. In exchange for purchasing goods out of a magazine, the girls had promised their classmates that they'd post photos online of Little Joe at camp.

The more Neeka talked to Val and Courtney, the more she realized how much they had in common. It was probably the first time they had ever talked about things that didn't involve sports. She was glad they were able to put aside their differences from last year. Part of Hickory Academy's difficulties the last two seasons had been its lack of teammanship. This year, they were already starting on the right foot. The girls seemed to be getting along. There didn't seem to be any hidden resentments.

Neeka just hoped it lasted.

****

The van came to a sudden stop, waking Payton from her sleep. She had been dreaming of dinosaurs and tater tots. Dinosaurs always seemed to be in her dreams when she was anxious or excited about something. Since joining volleyball, she'd had a lot of dinosaurs chasing her around at night.

As she lifted her head groggily, she noticed a drool stain on Neeka's hoodie. *Oops*, she thought, failing to remember how the hoodie had ended up under her head.

"We've stopped for lunch," Neeka informed her as the girls unbuckled their seatbelts.

Payton handed back her hoodie, but Neeka shook her head. "Who needs super soakers when we've got you? You can give it back to me when camp is over—after you've washed it." Her friend then jumped out and ran ahead to use the bathroom, along with Janette and Selina.

Stretching as she exited the van, Payton looked around. They had stopped at a small fast food place. She didn't recognize where they were exactly, but she reckoned they must be closer to Jackson than they were to Nashville. Beyond the highway, there appeared to be a stretch of farmland surrounded by big, bushy chestnut trees. It was a pretty sight. She almost regretted falling asleep during the drive.

Next to her, she overhead Courtney whisper to Val, "Do you think we'll be able to order what we want, or will the coaches be watching what we eat?"

Payton was amused by this. "The coaches are the ones who brought us here. You can eat what you want," she informed her.

Courtney rubbed her hands together eagerly. "Excellent. I'm craving a fried chicken burger and chili fries. YOLO."

Val flipped her hair, causing the sunlight to sparkle off her purple streaks. "I'll stick to a salad."

"Girl, you say that now, but we all know you're also going to order a super milkshake and brownie for dessert," Courtney countered.

"Why do you think I order a salad as my main course? I have to fit my veggies in somewhere."

Payton followed them into the fast food place, hypnotized by Val's hair. It was like looking at the back of a retro tiger. "Your hair is cool, Val," she complimented. "What made you put purple streaks in it?"

"It was so bone straight and boring, just hanging there. I was sick of it. I wanted something more interesting."

"Your mom didn't mind?"

Val looked down. "My mom doesn't really care what I do. She's too busy trying to pay the bills."

Realizing she'd hit a sore spot, Payton knew she should change the subject, but she didn't want Val to feel alone in the matter. Payton could relate. "It's hard not having a dad around. Ever since my dad moved to Cincinnati when my parents split a few years ago, I've found being at home kind of lonely. My mom is always focused on her work. We have plenty of money, yet it still feels as though she would rather spend her time with four blank walls than with her own daughter. Your mom works so much because she has no choice. I'm sure she'd rather be spending more time with you. My mom doesn't have the same excuse."

Taking her words in, Val was about to respond, but Selina ran up and slapped her on the back. "Why so serious, girls? We're here to have fun!"

Val smiled at Payton, the conversation over, and left to join Courtney at the register to order. The staff behind the counter didn't seem at all thwarted by their big group. They had plenty of burgers and fries waiting. One of the coaches must have called ahead of time to warn them the team was dropping in.

After ordering their meals, the girls gathered around a cluster of tables in the back. They chatted away, united in the nervousness and excitement they felt over what the next four days would bring.

"We're really getting along, aren't we?" Payton uttered to Neeka as the group broke into a massive sword fight with their straws. "There's a real sense of camaraderie."

"Yeah, I was thinking the same thing earlier. It's such a relief. We'll never make it to State if we're our own worst enemies. So far so good."

Payton was glad to hear Neeka talk about State so favorably. At the end of the last season, her friend hadn't been so confident, not after the beating they'd taken from Cumberland Lake. Neeka must have changed her mind. "I know we're not as skilled as some of the other teams we'd be facing at State, but I really do think we'll win this year."

Neeka held a hand up. "I want us to get to State, but I'm still not convinced we'll win. I think we have to think realistically. Otherwise, we'll just be disappointed. It's like what Lacey told us last year—we have to look at everything we've accomplished so far and measure ourselves against that. We've made history at Hickory Academy. We helped bring home the team's first District and Regional trophies. We can't let all that disappear or be any less important if we don't win State. The volleyball program at Hickory Academy is only five seasons old this fall. We improve every year, but I'm not sure one volleyball camp is enough to suddenly make us better than all the teams who have defeated us so far."

Payton slumped forward, but she refused to let the dream go. "I know we have to be practical and stay grounded, but hope is all I have. You're the rock; I'm the roll."

Neeka put her arm around her. "That's why, bestie, together we make the perfect volleyball player."

It was late afternoon by the time Hickory Academy made it to Jackson University, a short drive from the "Jackson Welcomes You: We're Glad You're Here" sign at the city border. The campus was just as the brochures described it to be. Leafy, narrow trees lined the stone walkways that were interlaced throughout the university grounds. Some of the buildings were older than others, fusing past and present together. Payton thought they gave the campus a lot of character.

Somewhere among the classrooms and dorms, the school had three gyms. There was an older one that, though outdated, was one of the largest university gymnasiums in Tennessee. The newer gym was much more modern and had a smaller practice gym attached to it, but it wasn't nearly the size of the first one. Payton wasn't sure which one she was more excited to play in. She didn't care. She was just so happy to be here!

"This sure beats the community center," Selina said, referring to the day camp in Nashville the girls had attended in years past, not too far from their school.

Payton nodded her head, lost for words. Though she was happy to be here, she was also super nervous. Unlike nearly every other sport she played, where she made All-Star teams and played at State championships, she did not excel when it came to volleyball. Her one saving grace, the one thing that made her stand out, was her topspin jump serve. She was the only girl in her district who could do one. But here, that didn't matter. She couldn't hide her lack of skills behind one serve. The instructors here would see instantly that she was far from an all-round player. In fact, there was a great possibility she would be the worst girl at camp.

"Just breathe," Neeka instructed her, sensing her anxiety. "We're here to learn. All of us. You have nothing to worry about."

"Thanks," Payton said, relaxing.

"This is killer!" Selina exclaimed as the team followed the stone walkway that led to the sports complex.

Hanging in the narrow trees that guided their way, volleyball-themed banners highlighted the names of the schools attending the camp. Jackson Central. Templeton. Parnell. Lincoln. Leland. Bridgewater... There were so many. They stopped excitedly under the tree with the Hickory Academy banner. Strung from it were blue and green streamers.

"Totes amazing!" Courtney marveled.

Quickly, they pulled out Little Joe and took a photo of him under the tree. They posted it online next to the one of him eating a hamburger at the fast food joint.

At the end of the walkway, a huge registration table was set up on the grassy lawn that connected the old and new gyms. Over a dozen other teams, from towns all over the state, waited while their coaches signed them in. One team, with bags in hand, made their way toward what looked like dorm rooms that bordered the complex.

"Listen up," Coach Mike called, running a hand through his spikey blonde hair. "First I'll sign you in. Then we'll receive your dorm assignments. You'll have about two hours to unpack, then we'll meet back here for orientation. After orientation, we'll all go out to dinner before Coach Gina and I leave you, but we'll be at a hotel nearby. Over the next four days, we'll be checking in on you. I expect you to do Hickory Academy proud, both in your performance and your behavior."

"You'll be great!" Coach Gina added. "Don't be intimidated by the other teams. You gals worked hard with your fundraiser to get here. Enjoy it!"

After they were signed in, Coach Gina guided them into the dormitory. Their rooms were on the fifth floor, Block C, whatever that meant. Payton stood on her tippy toes as the elevator took them up, willing it to hurry. She'd gone to summer camp before, but there had always been camp counselors in the cabin with her. With the exception of a few volleyball instructors on the first floor, this was the first time she'd be staying somewhere overnight without an adult around.

Finally, they arrived at their floor. There was nothing spectacular about it. A long, linoleum hallway led to the shower area and bathrooms. On either side of the hallway were a series of wooden doors with metal numbers on them. But Payton wasn't interested in the lack of decor. This was freedom!

"Payton and Neeka, you're in here." Coach Gina pointed to the first room on the right. "The room farthest from the showers—unlucky to be you," Selina taunted.

"Selina and Janette, you're in here." She indicated the room on the left, just opposite Payton and Neeka.

Selina's face instantly fell.

Snickering, Payton and Neeka hauled their bags into their room and shut the door. It was cramped, way smaller than Payton's room at home. A bed was set lengthwise against each wall with a desk and dresser crammed at the foot. A strip of carpet hardly big enough for one person to walk down separated the two halves of the room, which smelled of old, cheap furniture. For a week at camp, it would do, but Payton couldn't imagine two people sharing such a tiny space for an entire school year.

"Just think, Neeka. In a couple of years, this will be us living away from home. We have to apply for the same colleges. I don't think I could survive living somewhere like this without you."

12

"I know," Neeka said as she zipped open her suitcase and pulled out her purple sleeping bag, a pillow, and a fitted sheet decorated with stars. She tucked the fitted sheet over the mattress of the bed on the right. "I just hope we can find a college with a good basketball program for you and NASA-type training for me."

Following her friend's lead, Payton pulled out her own bedding—all Titan's gear, Tennessee's football team, her heroes. "I'm sure all the big schools have good science programs." She sat down, abandoning her bedding on the floor. "I can't believe we're finally here! I have no idea what to expect. That scares me a little, but mostly I'm just really excited! And hungry!"

Neeka laughed. "You're always hungry, but I know what you're saying. I can't wait to see what tomorrow brings!"

CHAPTER 2

A loud, obnoxious noise blasted into the room, waking Neeka up. Coming from a million different directions, it sounded like an annoying she-bird crowing loudly. She was pretty sure it was music, but it was much too peppy to be called such, especially this early in the morning.

"What is that?" Neeka groaned, turning in bed.

Still half asleep, she threw her pillow against the door, hoping it would somehow convince the noise to go away.

"That's not going to help," Payton said, sitting up. "The music is blasting from the hallways. It's our wake-up call."

"Music? Is that what you call it?" She pulled her sleeping bag over her head.

Payton laughed. "You can't hate country music forever. You live in Tennessee. You're surrounded by it."

"Watch me," Neeka said, trying to mute out the invading country girl lyrics.

When the song was over, a new one by a different artist began to play. The song immediately caught Neeka's attention. Sung by a bluesy old man, the song was quite charming. Her head still under the sleeping bag, she opened her eyes and tapped her foot to the smooth, folksy tempo.

Suddenly, she felt a soft lump smack her. When she peaked over her sleeping bag, she saw Payton towering over her, holding her pillow up in triumph.

"You can't turn my own pillow against me," Neeka protested.

"I think I just did," Payton declared. "Now get up, snoring beauty. We've got a big day ahead of us."

"If you weren't so tall, you wouldn't be so confident holding that pillow," Neeka whined as she sat up and stretched. "How much time do we have before breakfast?"

"About forty minutes, so we need to hurry up and shower."

"Forty minutes? That's loads of time."

"Not when you're competing with a dorm full of girls for the showers."

As Payton predicted, by the time they made it to the end of the hallway, a long line of girls in flip-flops, pajamas, and holding every color of towel possible had formed.

"What genius decided to install only eight showers?" Neeka mumbled.

A few places in front of them, Selina stepped out of line. Holding a dark purple towel and wearing stark black pajamas, she joined Neeka and Payton at the back.

"Word has it the female locker room showers are open," she said in a low, secretive voice. "Want to do some recon?"

"That sounds illegal," Payton said.

"It means to gather knowledge, like spy work," Neeka explained. "I guess we'd better. Otherwise, we'll never make it to breakfast."

The girls headed toward the locker rooms, their flip-flops smacking against the linoleum floor. It was strange having to walk so far to the showers. At home, the only barrier she had between her and a bathtub full of steaming hot water was Jamari trimming his nose hairs.

"Can you believe we're going to be upperclassmen?" she said to the girls.

"Yeah, I'm really going to try to enjoy this year," Selina vowed. "Senior year will be stressful, dealing with college applications and the like. This is the year to have fun!"

"Speak for yourself," Neeka moaned. "I have to find a job."

"Yeah, me too," Payton said.

"Why you, Payton? Your mom is loaded," Selina asked.

Payton shook her hair out from her ponytail holder. "She wants me to learn responsibility and all that yap yap yap. But Neeka and I have already discussed it. We're going to get a weekend job at the zoo."

"Make sure they don't confuse you for one of the giraffes, the way you eat," Selina joked.

Leaving the elevator, they entered the lobby of the dorms and stopped, staring at the lawn outside that they had to cross to get to the locker rooms.

"Are we really about to go outside in our pajamas?" Payton asked. "I don't think we fully thought this through."

"It's only us volleyball girls. Plus, it's not like you're naked," Selina teased.

"Are we headed for the old gym or the new one?"

Selina looked uncertain. "I'm pretty sure I overhead the other girls say the one closest to the dorms, so it must be the old gym."

Braving the outdoors, they quickly made a run for the locker rooms. As they entered, it was obvious they weren't in Kansas anymore. Or Tennessee. The lights were dim, like the lights in a prison cell, and the floors slick. Green algae clung to the walls. The place obviously hadn't been cleaned in a very long time.

"We're going to need a shower after our shower," she objected, grossed out.

"I feel like I'm in some sort of horror film," Payton laughed. "Like the *Swamp Thing*."

"Classic horror, nice one," Selina applauded, kicking at the algae. "Maybe this stuff is radioactive and we'll become superheroes."

With great hesitation, the girls turned on the first shower. The pipes banged around, making several loud thuds, but water eventually came out.

Selina pinched her nose. "I'm going in," she said before pulling the curtain behind her.

"Don't melt!" Neeka shouted, laughing when Selina squeaked.

"If we survive this, we can survive anything," Payton affirmed as they followed Selina's lead and found showers of their own.

The stall Neeka chose looked almost decent, except for a big water stain on the tiles and what she hoped was a pile of dust in the corner.

"Thank goodness for flip-flops," she yelled out. "I thought we were wearing them to prevent athlete's foot. I never thought they'd also protect us from wildlife in the showers!"

As they showered, their laughter echoed across the empty shower room. *Freedom comes at a price*, Neeka thought, quoting something a history teacher had once said. *But at least we can enjoy that price together.*

When they were finished, they quickly rushed back out the door into the fresh air.

"I think I left my shampoo behind," Selina said, halting.

"Leave it. We survived the jungle once. We may not again," cautioned Payton. "I, for one, am getting up extra early tomorrow. Before the wake-up call."

From across the lawn, several extremely tall, lean girls walked toward them, towels and shower gear in hand, obviously headed toward the locker rooms. Neeka couldn't help but notice everyone in the group was black, like her. They seemed friendly enough, chatting away.

"Should we warn them?" Payton whispered.

Selina shook her head. "Why? They're the competition."

"But they're taaaallll," Payton insisted, drawing out the word. "Even taller than me. What if we end up facing them during a scrimmage? I don't want them to kill us cuz we didn't warn them about the jungle."

"Bring it on!" Selina declared. "I scrimmage against you all the time, and I'm not afraid. There'll be girls just as tall in State. We need to be prepared for anyone."

We need to be prepared for anyone. Neeka liked that. It was true. If they had any hope of getting to State, they had to be ready to face anyone at any time.

"Are these showers crowded too?" asked one of the girls as they met on the lawn.

"There is literally no one in there," Payton answered.

"Unless you count the wildlife," Neeka added.

The girl frowned. "That bad, huh?"

"Yeah," Neeka warned. "Hope you brought your gas masks."

Smiling at Neeka's joke, the girl shrugged her shoulders. "Guess we have no choice. Breakfast starts soon. I'm starved."

The girl speaking was nice, but Neeka couldn't help but feel the stares she was getting from the rest of the group. They were looking at her up and down.

I guess Payton, Selina, and I are a unique trio, Neeka thought, though something told her that wasn't the only reason she had their full attention.

****

"Mmmm... smell those sausages. You know what I call them?" Payton asked, inhaling deeply as they entered the cafeteria.

"I'm afraid to ask," Neeka said, grabbing a tray.

"The hot dog of the morning."

"I take that back. I shouldn't have asked."

Selina hurriedly cut in front of Neeka as they lined up. "I thought they'd be serving gruel," she said.

"And I thought you would have learned some manners by now," Neeka grumbled. "If you steal the last blueberry muffin, I'm never going to set for you again."

"Funny, because that's exactly what I plan to do. You snooze, you lose."

"Then good luck approaching those strikes without my help."

"You have to set for me. I'm one of the best hitters on the team. If you don't, Coach Mike will replace you with Janette," Selina said matter-of-factly as she grabbed the only blueberry muffin in the basket at the self-service station. "Looks like bran for you."

Neeka was about to comment when her nose caught hold of a delicious smell. "That's okay. I've found something better."

She pushed her way past Selina and approached the hot food station where two college-age girls were serving up mountains of pancakes, sausages, eggs, and bacon while dancing around to the radio in the background, obviously enjoying their summer job.

"The one thing that beats a blueberry muffin is blueberry pancakes!"

"With scrambled eggs and sausages," Payton added joyfully.

After being served, the girls joined their team at a long table near the window. For the most part, all the teams sat on their own, segregated from their competition, except for a few of the upperclassmen who recognized each other from camps past. A few hellos were shouted across the tables, but there was no intermingling. Being in their first year, Hickory Academy sat quietly, not knowing anyone. They were the new girls.

"I didn't realize we were supposed to wear matching T-shirts," Val hissed across the table at Neeka as they sat. "We look like a bunch of rag dolls compared to these teams. What should we do?"

"Calm down, chili pepper," Neeka said, used to the girls looking to her for guidance. "We have our jerseys for scrimmages. That's all we need. There's no rule about what we have to wear during the practice drills."

Courtney didn't look convinced. "I'm with Val on this one. Matching T-shirts at camp are a sign of team unity. We should have thought to coordinate."

"Next time," Neeka said. "Just be glad we're here. It was hard enough raising money for camp, let alone matching T-shirts."

The truth was, Lacey Knox always thought of these things, like matching T-shirts, but she'd graduated last year. Now, she was playing volleyball for a university out of state, far away from Hickory Academy. Neeka made a mental note to make a list of other things her friend had been responsible for. It made her miss Lacey even more than she already did.

"Actually, I thought raising money was quite easy and fun... oh yeah, and it was my idea. You guys were so ready to give up on the whole overnight camp idea—"

Neeka cut Selina off by stealing a piece of her muffin. "We don't need a replay."

Val moved her food around her plate, barely touching it. "I hate the idea of all of us being split up today. I mean, isn't this camp supposed to make us better all-round players? Why do we need to be split up by what positions we play?"

Neeka felt bad for Val. As the only *libero* on the team, Val would have to brave the first day of camp alone. Neeka had Janette and a JV recruit from last year who was starting to show promise as a setter. The remaining girls on the team were hitters, those responsible for getting the ball over the net and scoring points.

"We'll all meet up again after lunch," Neeka reassured her. "Until then, just try to learn everything you can about being a *libero*."

"What else is there to know? I can replace whoever I want in the back row, so when all y'all are messing up, the coaches send me in to dig those balls out of the gutter and save the day. I'm kind of like Super Girl."

"Super Girl doesn't have purple streaks in her hair."

"She does now."

"The instructors seem pretty okay," Payton commented, her mouth full of pancake. "Coach Murphy is a bit intense though. He reminds me of Pharrell Williams, if Pharrell Williams were a volleyball coach for a zombie army."

"Did you see the size of him?" Courtney's eyes bulged. "He's even taller than Coach Mike! And he's bald, so it's not like his hair is making him any taller. Where have we entered into—the land of giants? I mean, everyone here is so freak'n tall!"

"He looks demanding, but fair," Neeka speculated. "It's a good combination. I'd prefer Coach Murphy to Coach Hopkins. She's working with the setters. At orientation last night, she sounded a bit overly strict. She kind of reminds me of my ma. Looks like her too, kind of. Different hair style, same serious expression."

"Maybe your ma was cloned?" Selina suggested.

"I'm serious!" Neeka said. "This is my first real taste of independence. I love my ma, but I didn't come all the way to Jackson to spend the day being drilled by her clone."

"Unless your mom is the clone, and Coach Hopkins is the original," Selina pushed.

Payton put her hand on Neeka's arm. "Don't worry, jelly bean. I'm sure Coach Hopkins will be fantastic."

****

The wisdom of Valerie's words regarding the matching T-shirts came to light as Neeka stretched prior to the start of setting practice. They were in the small gym, but even it was spacious. Poor Val had been stuck marching over to the old gym. Neeka hoped the gym floors were cleaner than the showers in the locker rooms.

"Hey, spirals, what school you from?" asked a bubbly blonde girl in a purple Lincoln High School T-shirt, bounding over to her.

For some reason, this caught the attention of the other setters, and they gathered round. Neeka shot a look at Janette, but she just shrugged, as did the sophomore next to her.

"Hickory Academy," Neeka answered. "Same as those two girls over there."

The blonde had a blank look on her face. "I literally have no clue where that is. You sure y'all are from Tennessee?"

"Actually, Hickory Academy is in Nashville, near the downtown area."

"You sure?" asked a girl with fiery red hair and freckles. "My two cousins live around there, and they don't attend Hickory Academy."

"We're a private school," Neeka clarified.

She could almost feel the air around her recede as the group pulled in one huge collective breath and answered, "Oh."

It was an odd response, but Neeka shook it off. She wasn't surprised they'd never heard of Hickory Academy before. It's not as though the team had statewide recognition... yet. If their response did anything, it fueled an ambition to make sure that, come this time next year, everyone in Tennessee knew who they were, with or without matching T-shirts.

Thankfully, Coach Hopkins chose that moment to address the setters, breaking the awkward silence that had fallen upon them. She stood upright with her arms folded and feet apart. Neeka took an inward breath, preparing for what would likely be a long, drawn-out day.

But to her surprise, the tone in Coach Hopkins's voice was a lot mellower than she had expected from the woman's steely exterior.

"Welcome to the setting drills," she greeted them. "As you know from orientation, I'm Coach Hopkins. I expect a lot from you today, ladies. I won't tolerate any laziness on my court. You're here to learn. I'll make darn sure you do. But I also want you to enjoy yourself. Volleyball requires heart. If you stop having fun and lose heart, there's no point playing. So follow my instructions today, show me some heart, and we should get on just fine."

To begin, Coach Hopkins asked them to spread out and simulate setting overhead. Bending her knees slightly, Neeka formed the shape of the ball with her hands and placed them in the air just above her forehead. Then, pretending her hands had just made contact with the ball, she extended her arms out.

Coach Hopkins observed, shouting out corrections and encouragement to the girls. "Great job, Leigh, but watch those wrists when you flick out. Keep them forward. Most of the control is in your wrists. Careful you don't spin the ball by letting your wrists go sideways."

I never do, Neeka thought, but kept her mouth shut.

"Okay, now freeze," Coach Hopkins yelled.

As commanded, all the girls froze in place. Neeka had her arms halfway extended out. Next to her, Janette still had her hands near her forehead, her fingers slightly curled as if receiving the ball.

"Does anyone else feel as if they're pretending to be a scary monster?" Janette joked, squeezing her claw-like fingers.

Coach Hopkins walked around, inspecting them. "I'm going to call out a checklist. If you fail to meet any of the criteria, please go stand by the wall. I can see all of you clearly, so no trying to fool me. First, are you square with your target?"

Was that a trick question? Neeka thought. None of them had a target. There were no balls out yet.

No one moved.

"Good," Coach Hopkins said. "Are your knees bent?"

Two of the girls went to stand next to the wall.

"Always be ready to spring to your feet, even when you're stationary. You can't count on the ball always being passed onto you. Sometimes, you'll have to track it. When you're aligning with the ball, keep your hands in front of you. Let your feet make the adjustment."

She moved on. "Are you pushing through with your feet?"

Another few girls, younger looking ones, unfroze to go to the wall.

"The force of your set is in your legs. When pushing the ball through, transfer your weight from the back of your foot to your toes to help put the necessary power into your play."

Neeka had heard all this before. *All the basics.*

"Final question. For this one, I want you to shut your eyes." She waited until all the girls still frozen did as instructed. "Without opening your eyes, can you tell me who's standing behind you? You don't have to know her by name. You just have to know what color T-shirt she's wearing."

Neeka quickly wracked her brain. Janette was beside her. Their sophomore teammate was diagonal to her. But no, she could not for the life of her recall who was standing directly behind her. Opening her eyes, Neeka reluctantly walked to the wall, as did a majority of the girls.

For the few still frozen on the court, Coach Hopkins tested them. One girl had it easy. No one was standing behind her. The other girl got it wrong and was sent to the wall. The final girl knew her teammate had been behind her.

Coach Hopkins called them all back onto the court. "Remember, you lead the team's offence. It is up to you to decide what hitters are in the best position to make the kill shot. You don't always have to know what hitter you're going to send the ball to, but you do need to know what area. To make that decision, you have to remain vigilant, constantly aware of what's happening around you. Any questions?"

When no one raised their hand, she blew her whistle. From the equipment room, two assistant instructors appeared, each wheeling a hammock-style ball stand. Based on their embroidered polo shirts, Neeka guessed they were from the Jackson University girls' volleyball team.

Coach Hopkins continued speaking. "Not only do you have to know where people are, you have to know what set will work best. For the most part, you will do the high overhead set we just simulated, also known as a four, to your outside hitters. But you have to be versatile. At times, you'll want to expedite your attack, make it quicker, particularly when working with the middle hitter. To do so, you'll want to set low.

This leaves less time for your hitter to make an approach, so make sure they're ready for it. We call this set a one."

For the next twenty minutes, she had the girls partner up to practice their overhead sets and their low sets. One girl passed the ball while the other set it back to her. As they did, Coach Hopkins again made the rounds, watching the girls practice.

"Well done, Leigh," she said when she reached Neeka and Janette. "Continue to keep your hands soft on that low set, and you've got it."

Neeka realized her earlier perception of Coach Hopkins had been all wrong. The woman was a mix between Coach Mike and Coach Gina. She got on their cases when she needed to, but she was also supportive.

When they were finished, the assistant instructors moved one ball stand to each end of the net. They then took a place next to the stands, clearly knowing what drill was coming next.

"If the ball is passed successfully to you, and you can build an attack," Coach Hopkins began, "more often than not your body will be facing the left-hand side of the court, parallel with the net. In this case, you either set a four, a one, or some other forward facing set. But depending on the circumstances of the play, the outside and middle hitters won't always be your best choice of offense. At times, you may have to back-set, delivering the ball to the area behind you where the right-side hitter is. This isn't always out of necessity. You may do it to throw the other team off guard, push them out of their comfort zone by doing something unexpected."

To demonstrate the motion of the back-set, Coach Hopkins bent her knees and put her hands above her forehead, but instead of extending her arms slightly foreword, she instead extended them straight up while pushing her hips forward, causing her back to arch just a tiny bit.

"See how I'm pushing my hips forward? When you back-set, use your hips to send the ball back, not your arms. Keep your arms high above your head and push the ball straight up. Your hips will do the rest of the work. This set is called a five."

Again, she gave the girls time to partner off and practice their back-set. This time Neeka worked with the sophomore. When they reconvened, she had them line up behind the back line.

"So now we have to combine vigilance with versatility. One by one, you'll take a setting position next to the net. As I pass the ball to you, I am going to call out either a four, one, or five. Using my assistant instructors as your targets, you will then perform the set I shout. This is a rapid fire drill, so as soon as you finish setting one ball, get ready for the next. I'm putting your coordination and accuracy to the test."

While each girl took their turn at the net, the other setters sat back and chatted away, mostly to their fellow teammates. Neeka decided to watch and absorb what Coach Hopkins was saying to the others. She knew she could learn from their mistakes. But it was hard to hear with the drum of the conversations around her.

When her turn finally came, she stepped confidently out onto the court, certain she could handle the pressure of the quick fire drill. As soon as she took her position, she realized the noise of the other girls had died down a bit. Most of them were studying her.

Sizing up the newbies, Neeka assumed.

But as she started the drill, setting with great accuracy every time Coach Hopkins called out a number, the quiet turned to silence. She had the full attention of everyone in the gym. It didn't bother her. She knew it was only because she was good.

You won't forget Hickory Academy now, she thought gleefully.

CHAPTER 3

"Have we entered a parallel dimension where everyone else is taller than the average human?" Selina asked her as they lined up for their first drill, along with the rest of the Hickory Academy hitters.

Payton wasn't really sure what to expect from the practice, especially as six girls in Jackson University polo shirts took position on the opposite side of the net, but she was glad they had ended up in the new gym. It was bright with a lot of natural sunlight streaming in from the high windows. Basking in the sunlight, she could almost pretend she wasn't about to make a fool of herself in front of the entire camp.

"Probably," she answered.

Courtney, usually so poised, shrank slightly. "That's not comforting, especially coming from you."

Payton understood their concern. They really had entered the land of the giants. The girls around them were beyond tall; a good few were over six feet. It was weird, having so many other tall girls around her. In a way, it freaked her out, but in another way, she liked it. But if the skills of these girls matched their height, going up against them would not be easy.

Selina took in the entire gym. "It's like we're surrounded by Amazons."

"The book company?" asked Courtney, confused.

"No," Selina scoffed. "The legendary women warriors of Greek mythology. They had an entire hierarchy of queens. One, Penthesilea, fought to defend Troy during the Trojan War. What did they teach you over in California?"

"How not to be rude, for starters," Courtney retorted, straightening her posture.

Coach Murphy stepped in front of the group. A barrel-chested, powerful man, he was truly massive. *Maybe that's why these girls are so tall,* Payton theorized. *In past years at the camp, they've had to stretch their torsos out to see him.*

"Welcome to my domain," he bellowed out. His voice was like a fog horn, echoing loudly against the walls of the gym.

Courtney winced. "Ouch. I think I'm officially deaf."

"Too bad you're not mute."

Instead of taking Selina's jab personally, Courtney whispered, "You know what, I'm actually flattered you're coming down so hard on me, Selina. That means you think I'm competition. But it also means I'm growing on you as a friend. You're only this mean to people you can tolerate, and who can tolerate you." To emphasize her point, she hugged her.

Selina grinned, her face squished into Courtney's shoulder. "Don't think that doesn't mean I won't beat you on the court."

"I'd expect nothing less."

"In a minute, you'll begin the morning drill I've prepared for you," Coach Murphy informed them. "But first, I want you to know exactly what it means to be a hitter. Yes, you spike and you block, everyone knows that. But I want you to fully understand how important your role is. You are the core of your team. Everything that happens before the ball reaches your hands—a pass from the back row, the setter positioning the ball—it happens for you. You score the points that bring your team to victory. And for front-row hitters, your ability to block the ball means you are also your team's first point of defense. You are the golden girls."

Payton liked Coach Murphy. He had a gentleness in his light brown eyes. But she didn't understand how every word he spoke could sound so angry, even with his booming voice. The man was totally intense.

"I can't teach you until you teach me," he said, starting the drill. "I want to see if each of you has what it takes to be a Coach Murphy All-Star hitter. Most volleyball players are right-handed, so hit better on the left-hand side of the court. That's why I've asked you to line up here on the left. You're going to work on your skills as an outside hitter. But first, I want to see what you've got!" The last sentence exploded out of him.

"See those girls over there on the other side of the net? Those are the Coach Murphy All-Star defenders. And there," he said, pointing to a seventh girl Payton hadn't noticed before even though she only stood a few feet away, "that's Lindsay. She'll be setting for you. One by one, I want you take the ball and put it away. I'm talking kill shots. Don't give my defenders a chance to even think about touching the ball. I want to hear it hit the ground."

Payton was suddenly thankful they had chosen to stand at the back of the line. Why was he throwing them straight into the deep end? Didn't he realize some of the girls here weren't ready to go against college athletes? Why didn't they start with more basic drills, like passing?

"If your shot is blocked or dug out, then you go to the back of the line, but if you're able to make that kill shot, then remain in place and Lindsay will set to you again. I want you to keep your momentum going."

"So if we're lucky enough to actually score a point, we have to keep going? Shouldn't it be the other way around?" Selina whined. "What kind of drill is this?"

The other teams didn't look as worried as Hickory Academy. Payton soon discovered why. Coach Murphy blew his whistle, indicating for the first girl to step forward. She wore a red Jackson Central T-shirt.

Time to sink or swim, Payton thought grimly.

Lindsay served the ball, but instead of the Jackson Central girl making a mess of it, she approached the hit like an expert, taking four steps before jumping into the air. Forming a bow and arrow shape with her arms, she swung her back arm forward to strike the ball over the net. It went spiraling across the court, landing in the deep corner. A point.

"Now that's what I'm talking about! Let's see if we can get a repeat performance." Coach Murphy signaled for Lindsay to set another ball.

The Jackson Central girl managed another two points before moving to the back of the line. There was barely a sweat on her as she high-fived the teammate who took her place. The second Jackson Central hitter looked just as confident and eager to begin as the first.

I guess that's the difference between us and them, Payton thought. *The drill is set up this way because these girls want to be out there. They don't want to move to the back of line. It's a reward if they get to stay. We need to start thinking like that. That's how champions think.*

As more girls took their turn at the net, Payton was made even more aware of just how far behind Hickory Academy was when it came to their skills. Shot after shot was hammered toward the defense. Not every girl managed to score, but many did, and they did it well.

Payton was in shock. She was certain she could see dents in the floor. The girls had such speed and accuracy. They hit the ball exactly where they wanted it to go, but they also had force behind their punch. It was a hard combination to work out, and it was lethal.

After another hit that left the earth shaking, Payton turned to Selina and Courtney. *Are these girls for real?* She didn't have to say it out loud. They were all thinking it.

When their turn came, none of the Hickory Academy girls, including Courtney, who was by far the strongest hitters they had, could manage a point. There was no comparison. Hickory Academy simply could not compete. They were District and Regional champions, but they might as well be jellyfish compared to these girls; their skills were nowhere close to the same level as their fellow campers.

Why do I feel weirdly comforted by all this? Payton wondered. She knew she should be upset that Hickory Academy was out of the zone, but she wasn't.

Though she was naturally athletic, she had struggled to develop her volleyball skills. Every skill she did have, she'd had to work hard to learn. She'd always been the underdog when it came to volleyball, ever since freshman year. Selfishly, Payton smiled, thinking that Selina, Courtney, and the others finally had an inkling of the frustration she had felt over the past two seasons. In a way, it united them. Now, they would all have to work hard to get to the level required if they were going to make it to State.

However, she could see the fear and disappointment starting to build within her teammates. That wasn't what she wanted. They had to stay positive if they were to move forward. She wanted to quickly quash any doubts that would destroy their motivation.

"This is what we're here for!" she proclaimed. "So we're the underdogs. Who cares? It just means we're not expected to be the best on the court, not like at home. The pressure is off. Let's use that freedom to find our feet and rebuild. We'll be fine."

Courtney nodded in agreement. "We knew we weren't the best. That's why we're here. Might as well make the most of it."

"Can I get a woop woop?" Selina chanted, her energy building back up.

Their words attracted Coach Murphy's attention. "Now that's the type of teammanship I like to see. Hickory Academy, you're the first to make it onto Coach Murphy's All-Star team."

"Do we get anything?" Selina asked as Coach Murphy walked away, though he was still within earshot.

Payton nudged her. "Respect," she whispered.

"I'd prefer a medal. Or some candy."

After the drill was over, Coach Murphy thanked the six defenders and politely dismissed them, leaving only Lindsay behind, who ushered the hitters into a wide huddle. With so many of them, it was almost comical.

Coach Murphy stood in the middle. "I said I wanted you to teach me, and you have. I learned you've got motivation. You've got spirit. You're ruthless, and I like that!" He looked specifically at the Hickory Academy girls. "And you know the value of teammanship. There ain't no better lesson than that."

He turned more serious. "I also learned that there are some common flaws you all are making. Make sure that, if you're hitting from the outside, when you position yourself to strike, you keep a forty-five degree angle with the net. Don't limit yourself. By keeping a forty-five degree angle with the net, you have access to the entire court."

A girl raised her hand. "What if you're a middle hitter?"

"We'll get to that later in the afternoon. Now, when you're hitting the ball, lean forward. You want the ball to hit the ground as fast as it can. Leaning slightly forward when you're in the air forces the ball downwards, making it harder for the defense to dig."

He paused, waiting to see if there were any questions. When no one spoke, he continued. "Momentum, momentum, momentum people. Use those arms to get you in the air. To hit like a Coach Murphy All-Star, you have to have momentum in your game, and you have to have rhythm in your soul." He did a little side step dance to illustrate his point, causing the girls to break out into giggles.

"And finally, when you make contact with the ball, try to hit it at its highest point possible. It'll give you much more control of where the ball goes and how it behaves getting there."

His tidal wave of instructions unnerved Payton at first, until she realized his voice overshadowed his true intentions. He wasn't trying to be loud and demanding; he was merely trying to encourage them.

The rest of the morning practice was split into partner drills so they could work on fundamentals, like jumping, passing, and using the wrist to force the ball into a downward spiral. As Coach Murphy barked orders her way, she found strength in his words, knowing he was actually cheering her on. Every time she heard him roar, she felt she could hit harder and jump higher.

By the time they finished for lunch, Payton could already see an improvement in her game. *Well, as Dr. B always says, sometimes evolution does happen overnight*, she thought, thinking of her freshman year Biology teacher. Dr. B had been her mentor ever since he'd first helped her fight out the insecurities she had in volleyball. He was a soft-spoken man, the exact opposite of Coach Murphy, but she knew he'd be proud if she told him how well she was doing.

****

Lunch in the cafeteria was as good as breakfast was. Payton loaded her plate with a turkey sandwich, macaroni and cheese, and an orange juice. She wondered if it was against camp policy to go back for seconds once she was finished. She couldn't believe all this food was included in the camp fee.

"Kind of feels like we're at a hotel on vacation," she said as she sat down next to the girls.

But no one smiled. Instead, they pushed the food around their plates, miserable. Everyone except Neeka.

"What's up with this crowd?" Payton asked.

"Tough day at the office."

Val flipped her hair. "How can you two look so happy? Neeka, maybe I understand. But Payton, I heard the hitters took a beating out there."

"Yes, but it was terrific!"

Val looked at her, dumbfounded. "I don't get you, girl."

"I actually saw an improvement in my game. After only one morning session. I mean, that's why we came here, wasn't it? Not to be the best but to get the training we needed so that by the time the season starts in the fall, we can be the best."

"For someone who can barely find her way around a volleyball court, you speak pretty lively," Selina said, "but I get you. I was fighting out there harder than I ever had."

"Exactly!" Payton said. "And, for the record, I'm not the klutz on the court I used to be. I've improved a lot over the years. If I can do it, so can all of you."

Val smiled, relaxing. "I guess miracles do happen; you're proof of that." It sounded harsh, but it was actually quite affectionate, coming from Val. For the first time all day, the girl took a huge bite of food. "Man, this is good," she said. "Do you think they'll let us go for seconds?"

Payton laughed. "I was thinking the same thing!"

****

The afternoon drills for the hitters carried on about the same as the morning ones, with Payton and the Hickory Academy girls battling their hearts out, even though they were by far the worst girls on the court.

"Not terrible, just underdeveloped," Coach Murphy said to her at one point. It gave her a shot of confidence, along with the rest of the girls.

But when the final drill of the day came, they lost some of that courage.

He selected the six tallest hitters, all over six feet, and pointed them to the opposite side of the court. "Over there, ladies."

Having been to the camp before, the girls expertly lined up, side by side, only inches away from the net.

"Your worst enemies on the court are the blockers. If you don't deliver a kill shot, you at least need to get the ball past the first line of defense. But if the blockers get to the ball first, that puts your team at a severe disposition. You'll be on the immediate defense instead of preparing for your next attack. Our final drill today is simple. Get the ball past the blockers."

The blockers leered, up for the challenge.

"I would pray right now, but I don't think that's going to help," Courtney said.

Payton and her friends moved toward the front of the line this time, wanting to get the torment over with. The Lincoln and Parnell girls in front of them were half and half successful, which helped Payton calm her nerves a bit. Her mind was already in full gear, trying to figure out where she should strike, studying her enemies to find the gap that would allow her to score.

When she took her turn at the net, before she was even in her ready position, Coach Murphy barked, "I can see the wheels in your head turning. Don't overthink it."

Payton did her best not to. She tried to clear her mind, but as Lindsay set the ball, she felt her body tighten as her thoughts took over. *When I spike, I need to flick my wrist downwards, just like Coach Murphy showed us this morning...* She did what she had been trained to do, but the ball was easily blocked by the other girls.

As she turned away, Payton thought she heard two of the blockers whisper something about Hickory Academy, but she couldn't tell for sure. With Coach Murphy bellowing out his encouragements, it was hard to pick out anything else.

After a few more rounds, Coach Murphy changed up the blockers, moving Payton to the other side of the net. *Finally, something I'm actually pretty good at!* Besides her jump serve, which she couldn't wait to unleash later, even though she knew many of the girls here could do the same, blocking was her other almost-specialty. She had a few things she could improve on when it came to blocking, but not much.

That's what she thought, anyway, until she actually did it. Blocking at this level was harder than she realized. The spikes that came her way were deadly, but she managed to keep up with the other blockers, knowing there'd be a few bumps and bruises on her arms the following day.

When Selina came to the net, she looked overly confident, probably because Payton was standing on the other side. *Keep your focus.* Payton tried to send the mental message to Selina. *Just because you're not going against the tallest girls anymore doesn't mean it's as easy as the other girls make it look.*

Her message went unheard. Selina pounded the ball over the net, but though it was powerful, she had no aim, and the ball bounced effortlessly off the palms of the middle blocker.

Selina didn't handle the outcome well. Her face lit up in anger. She looked really mad, more at herself than anyone else, Payton knew. Then the anger turned into determination.

"That's it, Selina!" Payton yelled. "Convert that energy to your advantage!"

Out of the corner of her eye, she saw Coach Murphy smile, but he said nothing.

It took a little while, with a few rotation of blockers in between, but by the end of the day, both Selina and Courtney managed to get their spikes past the blockers. Payton hadn't been so fortunate. She was the only one who failed to get a single ball over. She didn't let it dishearten her, not like it would have in the past, but she did feel slightly disappointed, no matter how hard she tried to shake it off.

"Time to eat!" Selina said, trying to cheer her up. "That's always your favorite time of the day."

Payton put on a fake smile. "Maybe they'll serve hot dogs tonight."

"Or sushi. I'd love some sushi," Courtney said.

As the girls headed toward the side exit of the gym that led back toward the dorms, Payton tried to stay positive. She had done a great job at blocking. That was good. And, overall, she still felt her skills had improved. Maybe not enough to make a kill shot, but enough that she felt she could continue working on her skills so she could improve even further.

"Moore, a minute of your time," she heard Coach Murphy shout. At least, she thought it was a shout.

Payton turned around. He stood near the net, waving her over with his clipboard. "Think he's gonna kick me out so soon?" she only half-joked to her teammates.

Without answering, Courtney pushed her forward before leaving with Selina.

"Yes, Coach?" Payton said, walking over to him.

He's face was neutral. "You know those girls were trying to stop you?" he said, matter-of-factly.

Payton was slightly confused by the comment. They were trying to stop everyone, weren't they?

"Yes," she answered.

"Why didn't you try to put the ball through them?"

She looked down. "I tried."

He used his clipboard to lift her chin back up. "I heard the way you talked to your teammates today. You've got the fever, child. Now put all that passion spewing out of your mouth into the game. Stop overthinking every little move. Get out of your head and bring out that inner fire!"

"But isn't half of volleyball analyzing your opponent, knowing where to hit?"

"There's a difference between making a quick decision and lingering on the details. You won't get the ball where you want it to go if you don't have a little spice in your punch. I'm talking speed and power. But your thoughts are holding you back."

To her surprise, he hunched forward and rounded out his arms to the point his knuckles almost touched each other, like the Hulk when he was angry. "Now repeat after me," he boomed, raising his voice even louder.

"You're not going to stop me!"

Payton swallowed her laughter, knowing Coach Murphy was serious. She imitated his posture and shouted, "You can't stop me!" realizing afterward that she got the words wrong.

"You sounded like a little mouse. Do it again. With fire. You're not going to stop me!" he rumbled. She was sure her father could hear him all the way in Cincinnati.

"You're not going to stop me!" she screamed at the top of her lungs with such force her face went red.

Coach Murphy stood back, impressed. "That's it, girl, you've got the fire!"

****

"I've been my own worst enemy," Payton admitted to Neeka as they finished preparing for bed. They'd already washed their faces and brushed their teeth in the bathroom, thankful there were more sinks than there were showers.

Neeka was cuddled into her sleeping bag. "Are you talking in your sleep already?" she joked.

Quickly changing into her pajamas, Payton sat on the edge of her bed, facing her friend. "For the past two years, all I've done is compare myself to other teammates. I don't do it quite so often anymore, but I still do have my moments of insecurity. It's caused me to get lost in my own thoughts while I'm on the court. I haven't let my inner fire out, not like I do in basketball."

Neeka sat up, paying full attention. "It's strange hearing you say that. I find the ability to think through something a bonus in volleyball. I think it's why I'm so horrible at basketball, but I'm so good at volleyball. I can think in slow motion in volleyball. It helps me."

"I don't think we're talking about the same thing," Payton said. "It's not that I think in slow motion. It's more my mind goes in a million different directions. It throws me off and causes me to ignore my own inner fire. I'm so afraid of being technically correct, I don't put any emotion into my game."

"And this is why the field of sports psychology exists," Neeka confirmed. "Sports is as much about mentality as it is about physicality," she said, quoting her brother, who Payton knew would be studying sports psychology in the fall.

"Your mom seemed pretty bummed when she dropped us off. When will you see Jamari again?"

"He's going to come back for two weeks before his school officially starts, but he's already moved out. Half the stuff in his room is gone. I already miss him."

"Me too," Payton admitted. Jamari was like a brother to her too. "We'll have to call him as soon as we get back from camp."

Neeka smiled a lopsided smile, straining not to cry. Payton hadn't realized before how much Jamari's move had affected her.

She got up and turned out the light. "Let's go to bed. Tomorrow's another day."

"Night," Neeka said from somewhere in the dark.

"Night, jelly bean," Payton echoed.

CHAPTER 4

"Are you seriously going to chance death again?" Selina asked Neeka as they stood in the hallway outside their dorm bedrooms. She yawned. "Isn't this why we got up super early?"

"Everybody got up super early. If I shower in the dorms, it'll have to be a quick one so the other girls in line don't whine."

"Speak for yourself," Selina said. "I'm taking my time."

Neeka wouldn't have thought otherwise. "I just want a long, peaceful shower. My muscles are sore from yesterday. They need lots of hot water. And I just need to zen out."

Selina shook her head, walking away toward the showers down the hallway. "See ya on the other side."

Gathering her shower supplies, Neeka went to the locker room showers across the lawn. To her surprise, when she arrived, there were already a few showers in use. Wondering who was in them, Neeka stepped into an empty stall and pulled the curtain closed. The place was cleaner than it had been the day before. Perhaps the janitors at the school had caught on that the campers had found the forbidden shower room. The algae was gone, but there were still water stains everywhere.

Before turning on the water, Neeka took a moment to put on her shower cap. As she did so, she heard the others leave their stalls.

"That was the scariest shower I've ever taken!" one of the girls laughed.

You should have been here yesterday, Neeka thought, tucking her spirals into her cap before reaching for the water spout.

"I heard the Hickory Academy girls were down here yesterday," another girl, one with a really deep voice, said.

Neeka stopped, leaving the water off as she strained her ears. Their conversation had just gotten a lot more interesting. They obviously didn't know someone else was in the room.

"Really?" the first girl asked, sounding doubtful. "I can't imagine those rich, private-school girls showering in here. Wouldn't it be below them or something?"

A third girl laughed. "Please, Mr. Butler, can you clean my spit from the bathroom sink?" she said in a mock posh accent.

Neeka clenched her fists, fuming. She wanted to let them have it, but besides the fact she only had a towel wrapped around her, she needed to learn more about what they thought of Hickory Academy.

"Their school has only played four seasons so far, yet somehow they've miraculously made it to Sub-State the last two years," said the one with the deep voice. "If they were any good, I'd believe it. But did you see how terrible their hitters were? There's no way those girls got to Sub-State on their own. I'll tell you what happened. They bought their way to the championship."

"They so did," the third girl said.

The first girl, at least, wasn't entirely convinced. "They just lost a lot of their players to graduation. I think a majority of their team this year were all on JV last year. And I heard their JV team was one of the worst in their district. It could be that all the good players left."

"No way. Girls that terrible do not make it to Sub-State, no matter how good or bad their JV team was last year. With all their millions, those girls can buy whatever they want. They bought their way to Sub-State. What's to stop them from buying their way to the State trophy this year?"

Neeka bit down on her lip to keep from screaming. *We made it to Sub-State because we worked hard, and compared to other teams in our own region, we are good!*

She badly wanted to defend her team, but she knew now was not the time. She was outnumbered, and nothing she said would make a difference. But that didn't stop the claims the girls were making any less ridiculous. A few girls on the volleyball team were attending Hickory Academy on scholarship, including herself and Val. So that no one felt singled out, the fundraiser they'd thrown had paid the camp fees of the entire team, including those who could have paid their own way. They'd worked really hard to come to Jackson University!

As soon as the girls left the locker room, Neeka took a short, agitated shower. Any hope she had of zenning out was gone. In her mind, she imagined slapping the girls on the back of the head with her wet towel, but she had no idea who had been talking or what team they were from. It could have been anyone.

****

At breakfast that morning, Neeka set her tray down hard on the table next to Payton and Val. "We need to talk," she declared angrily.

"Wake up on the wrong side of your sleeping bag?" Val mumbled.

"More like the wrong side of the showers," Neeka whispered, looking around.

Payton frowned. "What's the matter, jelly bean?"

Neeka speared her pancakes and then leaned in close, causing her teammates to do the same. She didn't want the teams around them to hear. Though, if she had it her way, she would stand on her chair and shout out loud how wrong they all were. Keeping her voice low, she told them what happened in the showers.

"If we find out who they are, I'm going kick their—" Selina began to say, but Neeka cut her off.

"None of that. I didn't tell you girls so that we could cause trouble and make an even worse name for ourselves. I have a feeling they aren't the only ones here who think we're some spoiled rich girls."

"What should we do?" Val asked, looking around, clearly upset. "They're all judging us, and it's totally unfair. I'd say a majority of these girls have more money than I do. I mean, the house I live in is no bigger than this cafeteria."

Janette seemed the calmest of all of them. She moved her long, blonde hair out of her face before speaking. "It's just misinformation. They don't know a lot about us, so they're speculating. It happens. We just have to make friends with them. When we're talking with them, somehow bring up how we had to fundraise to be here. Word will soon get around that we're not a group of rich brats."

Courtney looked indignant. "But some of us are rich. That doesn't make us brats."

Janette rolled her eyes. "That's my point. Show them otherwise."

"Selina isn't rich, not wildly anyway, but she sure is a brat," Val said playfully, though she still seemed distraught at Neeka's news. "How are we going to contain her?"

Selina stuck her tongue out. "You aren't. I don't care what these girls say about us. If you go around trying to please everyone all the time, you'll waste your breath. It's impossible. People will always find a reason to talk."

Neeka was impressed. Underneath all that eye make-up and rebel attitude, Selina really could be wise sometimes. But though she saw the intelligence behind Selina's words, she knew it would do nothing to help them get through the rest of camp. "I think both Selina and Janette are right. We need to stay strong and not let the rumors get to us, but we also need to do some damage control. Make friends. Let them know about the fundraiser."

The rest of the team nodded in agreement, but breakfast felt a lot more claustrophobic than it had the previous day. They kept looking around their seats, knowing the rest of the girls at camp were watching. And judging.

****

And?

41

That was Jamari's only reply in his text.

Neeka nearly strangled her brother through the phone. Didn't he understand that she really needed his help? This wasn't a time to joke. During breakfast, she'd texted him the situation regarding what she'd heard in the showers, hoping he'd offer further words of wisdom regarding what they should do.

She quickly sent another text. *Thanks for being so helpful, bird brain.*

I am be'n helpful. U go to a private school. People will always think that way about u. Get used to it and move on.

So he wasn't joking. He was serious.

What should we do?

Have fun.

Putting her phone away, Neeka stepped into the classroom where Coach Mike was holding a meeting before their second full day of camp. As soon as all the girls were present, the meeting began. Coach Mike, as usual, was wearing khaki shorts and a Hickory Academy polo shirt. He paced as he spoke.

"How did you ladies find the specialized drills yesterday?"

The girls collectively mumbled a half-hearted, "okay."

"Just okay?" He didn't look pleased.

Janette raised her hand. "Neeka did a fantastic job. Coach Hopkins kept using her as an example of what to do during the setting drills. She's kind of the star of the show."

Neeka blushed. She hadn't wanted to make a big deal of it.

"That's good to hear, but I'm not interested in one star player. We're here to improve. All of you should be putting yourself out there, challenging yourselves. I don't care if you're the best on the court, but I do expect you to be enthusiastic about what you're doing and to fall asleep every single night you're at camp knowing your game is stronger, even if only a little. That won't happen if you're comparing yourselves to the other teams. So I'm going to ask you again, how were the drills yesterday?"

"Great!" the girls shouted, though most didn't look so convinced. Afterward, the room instantly went silent.

Coach Mike looked around suspiciously at the grey atmosphere.

"That's... better. Now, as for today, you're back together as a team. You'll have a few team drills in the morning and part of the afternoon. They'll be things you already know, but that doesn't mean I don't want you working hard. The basics of volleyball are the most important. There's no point having an awesome serve if you can't also pass and spike. Listen to the coaches. Learn from them."He looked around, but the girls remained quiet.

"Starting tomorrow you'll scrimmage with another team. We'll know who you're playing later. Some of these girls are State champions. It'll be hard, but don't let that get you down. I want to see you fight out there. You're warriors. Don't surrender."

Again, the room was silent.

Coach Mike folded his arms. "Okay, what the hillbillies is going on here? Why are you gals so grim?"

The girls looked away, none willing to speak.

"We're not leaving here until somebody tells me what's up."

"Ask Neeka," Selina said.

"Neeka?" Coach Mike prompted.

Neeka drew a breath, already knowing what Coach Mike would say. He'd tell them to suck it up, just like Jamari had. But she told him anyway: everything she'd heard in the showers, specifically the part about Hickory Academy buying their way through the championship, and everything the girls had discussed at breakfast.

"You're not here to worry about what the other teams think of you. You're here to focus on your individual skills and your skills as a team. Volleyball is a competitive sport. Don't be foolish enough to think you're the only team being bad-mouthed at camp. All the teams here view all the other teams as competition, the team they might be playing at State. You're in the big leagues now, girls. Get used to it. Let the other teams think whatever they want."

"What's the point of winning if everyone just thinks we bought our way?" Courtney moaned.

Coach Mike almost looked offended by her words. "Because you still know the truth. And the only opinion that matters is your own. Listen, if you're that worried, prove them wrong. Get out there and work until your feet have wings and your arms turn to steel. Show them that Hickory Academy earns everything it gets."

The girls nodded their heads solemnly.

If Coach Mike can't get us pumped up, I'm not sure what will, Neeka thought.

****

Hickory Academy was definitely not having fun.

They were all in the old gym. Four volleyball nets were set up down the center. Having divided all the teams into smaller groups, their first team drill of the day was a back row exercise, where two girls at a time at each net stepped forward. A ball was served to either one, who then had to dig the ball and pass it to the second girl, who set it for a target hitter, marked by one of the Jackson University volleyball girls.

Hickory Academy had been joined with Parnell and Bridgewater in their group. Though they were working with them, and not competing against them, it was clear neither of the two other teams had any interest in getting to know Hickory Academy. They snubbed them anytime one of the Hickory Academy girls tried to make conversation while waiting in line for her turn at the net.

It made the Hickory Academy girls tense, all of them. It was hopeless. They wanted to prove themselves to the other girls at camp, but it was clear their skill level was simply not up to par. Even Payton, who usually told the worst jokes when she was feeling the strain, was quiet. It wasn't good. Lost in thought, the girls weren't communicating the way they should have been. Every time the ball dropped during a pass or set, Neeka couldn't help but feel they were proving the girls in the shower right.

She desperately wanted to earn the respect of the other teams, but she wasn't sure how they could do it. Not if they kept playing this way. She suddenly regretted telling the girls what she'd heard in the showers, though she supposed it was only a matter of time before someone else overheard something.

"Mine!" Selina shouted when the ball was served in between them, but Neeka heard her too late and they ran into each other.

The rest of the morning proceeded the same way. They didn't play horribly, but they definitely weren't at the top of their game. Neeka knew she had to do something to change their spirits. She'd caused this, so she was going to fix it. Quickly, she sent Jamari a text.

To her delight, he'd done what she asked by lunch.

As the girls sat at their usual table in the cafeteria, Neeka took out her phone and showed them a quick video. In it, Jamari and his new college buddies were dressed in homemade cheerleader costumes. It looked like one guy even had a lamp around his waist. Waving pom poms made of mop heads, the guys hilariously chanted, "We've got spirit, yes we do. We've got spirit, how about you!!! Go Hickory Academy!!!" At the end, they broke out into what could only be described as a very uncoordinated dance.

By the time the video was finished, the Hickory Academy girls were laughing so loud, there was no doubt that the entire lunch room was looking at them.

"That will totes go viral!" Courtney exclaimed.

"Better not let the Hickory Academy cheerleaders see. They'll go running for their money," Val added, her face red from laughter.

Next to her, Payton snorted repeatedly, unable to speak.

The video had the desired effect. By the time the girls were back on the court, her teammates were in much better form. They spent the afternoon practicing their jump serves. Payton oversaw the drill, helping her team improve their techniques. Most of the balls landed in the net. It'd be a while before the other girls could actually perform a jump serve, but they had all summer to practice. Instead of despairing, they happily clapped and cheered each other on. But there was a hidden intensity behind their cheers, like anger.

Anger is a good thing, Neeka decided.

Where there is anger, there's a fight.

CHAPTER 5

"I can't believe you're finally letting me do this!" Courtney exclaimed to Payton as she hurried to her backpack and pulled out her container of beads. "I've been wanting to put cornrows in your hair for ages!"

Payton took a seat in a desk chair. "Well, now's your chance." She was excited as well. She wanted a change, something new to make their first overnight volleyball camp experience completely memorable.

"You know your mom is going to make you take them out the minute you get home from camp," Neeka warned.

Selina huffed. "Beats getting a tattoo."

Payton ignored them both and sat back to let Courtney do her magic. They were in the dorm room she shared with Val, but Val was outside having a long chat with Stephen on her phone. Courtney had invited them over, knowing Val's conversations with her boyfriend could last hours.

"They okay?" Payton asked with concern.

"Who? Val and Stephen? They're great. Why do you think they talk for so long? They are in L.O.V.E."

"Yuck," Neeka said.

"You're one to speak. You ever gonna tell us who your secret crush is?"

Payton was surprised. Neeka had never mentioned a secret crush to her. That was unusual. Neeka told her everything. "You have a secret crush, Neeka?" she asked, trying not to sound as hurt as she felt for not being told.

Neeka looked instantly embarrassed. "No one worth mentioning. Just drop it."

A bit harsh, Payton thought. She couldn't remember the last time Neeka had a crush on someone. Maybe it was a boy band member who wasn't as cute as the others. Or maybe it was one of Jamari's friends, and she was worried about him finding out. Still... Neeka would have told her, even in those cases. This was strange.

"Gladly forgotten," Courtney said, holding a jade bead up to Payton's face. "Will I do your hair the same as my own? Jade will really bring out your green eyes."

Payton didn't know much about color coordination. "Go for it," she said, assuming that was the right thing to say. "After this, we need to get a photo of my hair over Little Joe, so it looks like he's the one with the braids."

"Did you see the photo Selina got of Little Joe with Coach Murphy? He was laughing so hard in the photo. He loved it!" Courtney told them.

"Yeah, it was pretty good," Payton said.

Standing behind her, Courtney gently pulled back a few strands of Payton's hair and began braiding them from the root.

"Does it hurt?" Selina asked, taking a seat on one of the beds.

"There's a bit of a pull, but no, it doesn't hurt."

"That's because I'm an expert," Courtney boasted. "But your head will feel a bit heavy, especially after all the beads are in. You have such thick hair. I hope I have enough beads to get through it all."

In the mirror on the desk, Payton noticed Neeka frown behind her. She didn't understand why Neeka was against this. Neeka was usually so fun-loving.

"It's not harming anyone," Payton reassured her.

"I'm not so sure of that," Neeka said. "What if you wake up with a sore head and can't play at our scrimmage against Leland High School tomorrow? Or what if your beads get in the way as you try to hit the ball?"

"We'll tie her hair back into a pony like I do," Courtney said, indicating it was no big deal.

"That won't stop her from waking up with a sore head."

Payton studied her friend carefully. "Are you worried about me, or are you more worried about how we perform tomorrow?"

Neeka looked down, unable to answer.

"We'll be fine," Payton reassured her again. "Leland is good, but they're not the best school here. They're not going to cream us."

"No, but they are going to challenge us. We have to be at our best. See how we measure up. We can't do that if you can't focus because your hair is too heavy."

Courtney stopped braiding. "The beads aren't going to be so heavy she can't jump. Her head will just feel heavier than normal, that's all. Look at me. I'm the best hitter on the team, and I wear cornrows all the time."

"You wish you were the best," Selina grumbled.

Neeka still wasn't pleased. "You're used to it. Payton isn't."

Payton could sense a standoff looming between the two girls. The last thing she wanted was an argument. She knew Neeka was overly stressed, but perhaps she had a point.

"Okay, how about Courtney just puts in two small braids, one on each side?"

Neeka looked relieved. "I do think that will be better."

Courtney undid the braid on top of Payton's head and started on a side braid. "You know, this is the first time Payton has shown any interest in hair. I thought you'd be more supportive. She finally wanted to be glam."

"I wouldn't call cornrows glam. Cool, definitely. But not glam," Neeka said.

Courtney turned toward her. "Girl, everything about me is glam." She went back to braiding Payton's hair. "I had high hopes Payton would be my new apprentice."

"Dream on," Selina said.

Payton laughed at their conversation. "Sorry, Courtney, but hair is my limit. You'll never catch me in make-up or nail polish or high heels."

"Famous last words," Courtney said with a knowing smile.

****

Payton stood on her tippy toes, trying to sec if by doing so, she would be taller than the Leland High School girls on the other side of the net.

No luck. Most of their opponents were still taller, the shortest on the team being over five-eight. They lingered about, waiting to line up before the start of the match.

It was their first scrimmage at camp. She and the rest of her teammates were nervous. Camp was going by so fast. It was already the afternoon of their third day. Somehow, she'd thought they'd be super players by now, but the reality was, they were only meant to learn new skills at camp so they could go home and practice them over the summer, ready for the fall.

It didn't mean that Hickory Academy didn't want to win any less. They were aching to show these girls all they had, to prove their worth.

"Please let us win," Payton said under her breath, staring across the net.

Coach Mike called them around the bench. "Remember to keep your focus," he ordered. "Earn their respect. Push hard and play well. Believe where others have doubted! You are strong! Show them the District and Regional Champions that you are!"

As Coach Mike continued giving them a pep talk, Payton looked up into the bleachers. The scrimmages were open to the public, so many of the locals were filing in to watch, along with a few college scouts. Thank goodness she didn't have to worry about that just yet. There weren't a lot of people in the bleachers, but enough to make Payton feel the pressure even more.

Celebrate the positives, Payton reminded herself, trying to stay optimistic. *At least I'm starting!* Coach Mike hadn't officially told her she'd be a starter this season, but being a starting hitter at their first scrimmage was a very good sign that she might. Courtney and Selina were also starting hitters, with Courtney taking the position of middle hitter and blocker.

"...You don't have to win to earn respect. You just have to give them a good fight," Coach Mike concluded with Coach Gina nodding in approval by his side.

"Bring some fire, right?" Neeka whispered to her.

"Right!" Payton said, remembering Coach Murphy's words that she needed to tap into her passion when she was playing. "Like a phoenix!"

Leland High won the coin toss and chose to serve first. Payton waited in her ready position, her knees bent and her hands up. As the Leland girls also got into position, she studied her opponents, deciding who their weakest link was. If she aimed the ball at their setter, then the girl might not have enough time to prepare the ball for an attack... Though Payton strategized, she tried not to let her thoughts get out of control. She fueled her body with her desire to win.

As expected from their drills, Leland used a jump serve to start the match. The ball came spinning at them, like it was barreling a hole through time and space, but Val dived for it, landing hard but managing to dig it out, passing it on to Neeka to set. Payton moved away from defense and prepared herself for the offense. It was clear Courtney had the best opportunity to score, so Neeka set the ball low to her area of the court.

Using a mighty punch, Courtney was able to send the ball flying past two blockers, but Leland got to the ball before it hit the floor and set up their own attack.

"Get ready!" Neeka shouted.

Hickory Academy were. They had to dig deep and strike hard, but they managed to keep the ball in play. After a while, with the locals, camp instructors, and coaches watching intently, Hickory Academy managed to score the first point of the match.

"And that's how it's done!" Selina yelled, throwing her first into the air.

"Calm down, Cho. It's only the first point," Coach Mike warned her from the sidelines.

The girls on either side quickly huddled. As Neeka shouted out encouragements, Payton let her eyes wander over to the other team. To her surprise, many of the girls glanced back at them, a look of shock on their faces.

Payton smiled. *Bet you were expecting us to go down from the start. Nope.*

She turned toward her team, interrupting Neeka. "We've gotten this far because we're not afraid to fight. Whatever you do, don't stop fighting."

It was a long battle that went all the way into the fifth set, the score close the entire time. In the end, Hickory Academy lost, but they weren't as bitter over the defeat as they could have been. They were happy they'd made the other girls sweat. For the first time since camp started, they felt they'd proven to their fellow campers just what they were made of.

We've come such a long way, Payton mused. *We really have.*

****

We still have so far to go, Neeka thought, and then said it to Payton as the girls used their seats at the bench to warm up for their final scrimmage at camp.

Payton obviously didn't hear her. "I can't believe camp is over today," she said. "I don't want to leave, but I also have to admit, I kind of miss my mom."

"I know the feeling," Neeka said, but her mind was elsewhere. She watched as the Jackson Central High School girls stretched their long muscular legs. The entire team was in top shape. Neeka mentally added overall conditioning to her list of things Hickory Academy needed to work on. Many students from Jackson Central, a local school, were in the bleachers to watch the match. The volleyball team had a big fan base. They'd almost won State the previous year. They'd even beaten Cumberland Lake in the semi-finals, the team that had destroyed Hickory Academy at Sub-State.

Initially, Neeka had been interested in seeing how Hickory Academy measured up next to the Jackson Central girls, but watching her opponents stretch, she knew there was no comparison. These girls had a presence, charisma. They screamed winners. That was something that only came with the confidence of being a superior team, something Hickory Academy couldn't rival.

From the first serve of the game, it was clear just how good Jackson Central was. The speed of their play was astounding. Though Hickory Academy dug the first serve out and returned the ball over the net, the precision with which Jackson Central responded and set up an attack was inspiring. Neeka couldn't help but be slightly in awe. They *were* better than Cumberland Lake. Way better.

The first point of the game was a kill shot, delivered by Jackson Central.

Neeka took a deep breath, gathering her strength. As Coach Mike had told them the day before, they had to show the other team they were a force to be reckoned with. They weren't to be doubted. She wasn't sure they could win, but they could prove they were championship volleyball players by showing off the skills they had used to win the collection of trophies that now lined the school's display case at home. Trophies that had been earned, not bought.

Trying to keep her body loose and her mind clear, Neeka banished all concerns about how good the Jackson Central team was as far away as she could. Instead, she concentrated on her own skills and the movement of the ball.

But the rest of the Hickory Academy team didn't keep their cool so well. As more shots were fired their way, and more points earned by Jackson Central, her teammates tried to overcompensate. Mimicking their opponents, they increased the speed of their play, but they weren't skilled enough to perform at such a level. It caused them to lose their accuracy, missing hits and sending free balls over to the other side, which made it even easier for Jackson Central to score.

"Don't play like Jackson Central, play like Hickory Academy!" Neeka shouted numerous times throughout the first and second sets.

It was useless. Her teammates were trying too hard to prove themselves. Even though they'd given Leland a good fight the day before, the way the girls at camp had snubbed them all week had gotten into their heads. Instead of performing well, their need to be as good as Jackson Central was making them sloppy, unfocused.

"Keep that inner fire but concentrate!" Neeka shouted to her team, hoping they would slow down and aim better. "It's a balance. Find it!"

Of the starting hitters, Courtney was doing the best. She was able to remain loose, to get her shots where she wanted them to go. Payton and Selina weren't having the same luck. Selina was too stiff, causing her to lock up. Payton was trying to put so much passion into her game, she had too much power and not enough accuracy. Several of their spikes were blocked, and Payton's timing was so off, she continually mishit.

It wasn't a slaughter. After Coach Mike gave them a stern talking to, and after Jackson Central's *libero* had to sit out due to a hurt shoulder after diving for the ball, Hickory Academy won the third set, but lost out on the fourth, losing the match.

Neeka had known they wouldn't win, but she felt that paired against Jackson Central, the Hickory Academy team were misfits playing in the big leagues. How on earth did they expect to get to State in such a short time? Volleyball season would start in September. It would be finished by October. That only gave them the rest of July and August to play like State champions.

It was no secret her thoughts regarding State had fluctuated since they lost against Cumberland Lake at Sub-State. Sometimes she thought Hickory Academy could make it all the way to Knoxville, where the State championship was held; other times she thought they should remain realistic and focus on Regionals.

If camp had proven one thing to her, it was that the girls did look to her as a leader. From mismatching T-shirts to scandalous allegations overheard in the shower, her team turned to her for guidance and support. They asked her for help at practices. They asked her to speak to Coach Mike on their behalf about any issues they were having. They even asked her advice when it came to matching hair ribbons to their jerseys. But more than anything else, her team expected her to lead them to State.

However, after playing against Jackson Central today, Neeka knew that was something she was not able to do.

CHAPTER 6

"Relax, you look like a grumpy old woman," Selina said to Neeka.

Neeka shook out her shoulders, coming to. "Sorry, I was deep in thought."

"None that were good by the looks of it."

Payton scrutinized her. "Everything okay, jelly bean? You seem kind of stressed."

Neeka leaned her back against the wall, trying to put on a fake smile, but she knew Payton saw through it. Sitting on the top row of the bleachers, they were supposed to be paying attention to the scrimmage in front of them. Bridgewater versus Templeton. The two teams were rival powerhouses, often competing against each other at State over the past couple of decades. Coach Mike wanted the girls to study them, to learn their strengths and weaknesses in case they ever had to play them.

We'd have to make it to State first, Neeka fretted. She didn't doubt Hickory Academy's dedication or hard work, but she did doubt their skill level. She now wished she'd never spoken of State in front of them. She felt bad, as if she'd given her team false hope. Sure, they could win Regionals, but if they were paired against any team with a skill level similar to Cumberland Lake's, then it wasn't likely they'd get past their Sub-State match, not this year. Maybe not ever. Hickory Academy was simply at a disadvantage. These other teams had girls who had been playing volleyball for years, ever since they were kids. Since Hickory

Academy Middle School didn't have a volleyball program, the only background she and her teammates had when it came to volleyball were a few PE classes. A small handful of the girls did play recreationally, like for their church group or country club, but nothing substantial. That left very few years to train the girls up to play at a competitive varsity level.

"She's gone again," Selina said.

Neeka was vaguely aware of Payton waving her hand in front of her face. "Earth to Neeka. Anyone in there?"

Neeka ignored them. Instead, she looked down at Coach Mike and Coach Gina sitting a few rows in front of them taking notes. She squinted to see what they were writing. Coach Mike's penmanship was impressively neat, but then Neeka remembered he was also the Creative Writing teacher. It was kind of his thing. She could just make out the words: *Buy wife an anniversary present.*

She shook her head, disgusted. *Great, even the coaches aren't taking this seriously. What hope do we have?*

Watching Bridgewater and Templeton play on the court would have been fun, if she didn't know that they could be paired against them one day in the not-so-distant future, if they did manage to get past their Sub-State match. Now, instead of admiring their skills, she felt threatened by them.

Hickory Academy wasn't the only team watching the scrimmage. The gym was pretty full. Many predicted this could be a preliminary match for the State final. A friendly match, so to speak, before the two powerhouses fought for the ultimate title. But the way the two teams looked at each other now, there was nothing friendly about them.

Neeka felt her stomach turn at the observation.

The team was perfectly focused. They spiked with power, speed, and accuracy, but they also dug the ball and passed to perfection. Each play was intense. It was no wonder the crowd around her was up on its feet cheering and whispering of a State final.

Then again, Neeka thought, *neither Bridgewater nor Templeton were in the final last year. It still could be anyone's season. Not ours. But any of the top teams.*

Though she knew they would likely never win State, Neeka wondered if Hickory Academy would ever be as good as the girls on the court below, enough to be considered a top team. It was possible, she decided. If Coach Gina started training the JV girls harder, got them to round out their skills, particularly their jump serves, early on. Maybe years from now they could be a top team in the state. But not now. Not this year.

As Coach Mike flipped his notebook to start on a fresh page, Neeka squinted again to read his notes.

Weakness: Overconfidence and the hearts of the fans. What that means for HA: Everyone loves an underdog.

****

After the final scrimmage and a closing camp ceremony where chocolate volleyballs were passed out as rewards, such as for Best Hitter and Most Enthusiastic Player, the teams had an hour to pack up their belongings and sign out. Selina had already packed up her stuff during lunch, so she followed Payton and Neeka into their dorm room. Neeka didn't mind. It gave them a chance to talk.

"There goes our freedom for the rest of the year," Selina moaned, slumping onto Payton's bed. She put a pillow over her head. "I don't want camp to end."

"I have to pack my bedding up soon," Payton warned her.

Selina didn't budge. "How long does it take to roll up a sleeping bag?"

Neeka laughed out loud. "If you thought volleyball was tough for Payton at first, you've never seen her roll up a sleeping bag. It takes her hours."

Sighing, Selina rolled off the bed, and in a surprising act of goodwill, began to roll up Payton's sleeping bag for her.

"So..." Neeka began as she re-packed her clothes. "I think it's time to call the first official meeting of Team Scary Pancake for the new season."

Team Scary Pancake was the name they'd come up with last year when Coach Mike had told her, Payton, and Selina that they'd be leaders on the team. They thought of it one morning after trying, very unsuccessfully, to make homemade pancakes by flipping them into the air. Her ma was still pulling batter off the oven fan. Only later did they realize how perfect the name was when they learned about the term pancake used in volleyball, where someone dived and threw their hand down flat on the ground, like a pancake, to keep the ball from touching the floor.

Agreeing to the meeting, Selina got up and shut the door. "Don't want any of the other girls to hear us while we gossip about them," she said before continuing to roll up Payton's sleeping bag.

"We are not going to gossip about anyone," Payton said. "That's terrible."

"Just joking," Selina said.

Payton looked her over. "With you, it's hard to tell."

Selina smiled proudly at the comment.

Neeka stopped packing and took a seat on her bed. This was serious and needed her full attention. The other two girls followed her lead.

"I just thought we should discuss where we are as a team," Neeka began. "Now that we've seen how other girls in the state play, we might want to reassess our goals."

Payton looked indignant. "Our goal is the same as it is every year. We want to win State."

Neeka scratched her head, choosing her words carefully. "But isn't that just setting ourselves up for disappointment?"

"No," Payton said, her voice growing quiet. "I don't think so."

"Neither do I," said Selina. "What's that saying? Reach for the stars and you'll land on the moon. We have to set a big goal, push ourselves to meet that goal, and even if we don't achieve that, we'll still have achieved something. Look at the last two years. We wanted to win State. And though we haven't even made it to State yet, we've still brought home two District and Regional championships. We did that because we had the goal of State in mind."

Neeka understood her point, but it didn't ease her mind. "Yeah, but that was before we discovered how good teams in other regions are. In my Careers class last year, we learned to make small, realistic goals that can be realized. That way we don't get discouraged."

"That's for when you're competing against yourself, like whether you'll have the motivation to build a jewelry case or something like that," Selina said. "This is sports. We're competing against others. The only goal should be the top trophy."

"Small goals are set to achieve bigger ones," Payton added. "In a way, we've already done what you've said. We set a small goal to earn respect from the girls at camp, and we have. Kind of. They know we aren't the best team at camp, but they've also seen our potential. They know we earned our championship titles. So now we keep making small goals, like you said, but with the ultimate goal being to win State."

This made perfect sense. For the first time since losing their scrimmage against Jackson Central, Neeka began to feel better. "I see your point. Camp was a good experience. It helped the girls see that we can still improve, even though we went undefeated during the regular season last year. It'll keep them on their toes, keep them pushing toward that next small goal."

"Every little bit helps," Payton agreed.

Something in her words struck Neeka. *Every little bit helps.* An idea began to brew. Neeka grinned, delighted.

"Why do I suddenly feel as if I'm witnessing a mad scientist at work?" Selina asked.

"Hear me out," Neeka said. "How about we recruit some new players?"

The shock on Payton and Selina's face was almost humorous, if Neeka wasn't totally serious.

"You mean like freshmen?" Payton asked.

"Yes, but not only freshmen. How about some of the girls on the basketball team? Or soccer? Anyone who is at all athletic but not already playing a sport in the fall."

Selina looked insulted. "Why?" she demanded.

"Why not?" Neeka countered.

Payton raised her hand. "Well, for starters, look at me. I was recruited from the basketball team. I'm an All-State basketball player, might I add. And look how well that turned out. This will be my third season playing volleyball, and I'm still having trouble spiking the ball over the net."

"It turned out fine," Neeka insisted. "You're a great blocker, and last year, you were the only girl in the district with a topspin jump serve. We won a lot of games because of Coach Mike unleashing that jump serve at the end of a match."

"No," Selina said, her voice full of authority. "Hickory Academy has never had try-outs. Not yet. That means anyone who wants to play can. Unlike years past, we've done a good job of advertising the volleyball program to upcoming freshmen and to others in our own school. Those who want to be here are here. Those are the girls I want to play with. We'll win with the team we have."

Payton nodded in agreement. "I'm with Selina on this one."

Neeka was about to point out that some passions were learned and some talents discovered, like the way she only joined the volleyball team because Payton didn't want to join alone. She never thought in a million years when she signed up for the JV team freshman year that volleyball would come so naturally to her or that she would enjoy it so much.

But seeing how stubborn Selina was being on the issue, she knew no matter what she said, the other two members of Team Scary Pancake would not support her on this.

****

It was night by the time the girls left camp. Everyone in the van was asleep, except for Neeka. And Coach Gina, of course. On the radio, Coach Gina had classical music playing.

It's no wonder everyone else is asleep, Neeka thought, listening to the slow, mellow tunes.

With Payton drooling once again on her shoulder, but this time with the hoodie secured in place, Neeka looked out the window to the night sky. Above her head, she spotted the constellation Ursa Major, the big bear. In Greek Mythology, which they had been required to study their sophomore year, they were taught that the constellation was named after the nymph Callisto, who was so beautiful, Hera, Queen of the Gods, turned her into a bear out of jealousy.

Maybe it's better to be a bear, Neeka thought, studying the stars above. *As a bear, I'd have unlimited strength.*

As intriguing as the stories behind the constellations were, she knew the true power of the stars was their ability to guide people. Not just in the horoscopes Courtney read to them from her fashion magazines. In history, before there were GPS units, people used to navigate their way around the world using the stars as markers.

That's what she needed to do as well. She needed to provide guidance for her team. Looking around the van at her sleeping teammates, she knew they believed in her, so she would believe in them. She would not doubt them again. She'd watch over them to make sure they were working hard throughout the season. Last year, she'd let the JV team off too lightly when they'd messed around. Pushing everyone now to do their very best was the only way she could make sure their hearts didn't break if they didn't make it to State. If they worked hard, then at least they could say they'd done everything they could.

CHAPTER 7

Driving in Jamari's jeep to her first day of school was bittersweet for Neeka. She loved the freedom of having her own set of wheels, though technically, Jamari got full control of the jeep whenever he came home to visit. But though it provided her with freedom, it also brought with it the stark reality that Jamari no longer lived with them. She may never again live under the same roof as her brother.

"I almost feel bad painting the jeep yellow," she said.

"Why?" Payton asked, sitting in the passenger seat next to her.

Neeka hadn't realized she'd spoken out loud. "Nothing. I'm just missing Jamari, that's all. He drove me bonkers at times, but he was also my rock."

"I miss him too," Payton admitted. "But at least he left you a fantastic going away present."

"Yeah, the jeep is pretty awesome."

Payton sighed. "I wish I had my own car."

Neeka tried not to smile. "But to have our own car, first you have to pass your license test."

"Don't think for one moment I don't see that smirk on your face," Payton said. "I daydream too much. That's why I'm a terrible driver."

"Failing your test three times doesn't make you a terrible driver."

"Yes, it does," Payton insisted, and they both burst out laughing because they knew it was true.

Neeka rounded a corner into the school parking lot. "Here we go, junior year."

"Ugh," Payton said. "I don't want to get out of the car. If I do, it means I'm officially in my third year of high school. It's all going by too fast. Our childhood is over."

"No need to be so drama-y," Neeka said, stepping out of the car. She patted down her plaid skirt and reluctantly put her blazer on over her polo shirt—the Hickory Academy school uniform.

Payton did the same, pulling at the black leggings she wore under her skirt.

"You know, girls can wear pants. Why don't you?"

"Because until boys can wear skirts, we're not truly equal."

Neeka laughed at the comment. She knew it was Payton's way of saying her mom was making her wear the skirt, though she didn't want to admit it. "I don't want to see any hairy legs!" she protested, imagining the boys in skirts.

"My legs are hairy."

Grabbing her backpack from the back of the car before locking the jeep door, Neeka said, "Payton, you can barely see the hair on your legs. Boys' legs are more like tarantulas."

Payton put a hand to her stomach. "Let's talk about something else; this conversation is making me queasy."

Neeka agreed. "Too bad we don't have our first class together, but it's cool that we have all the same afternoon classes."

"I'm especially excited for AP Biology," Payton said as they entered the school. "We'll be reunited with Dr. B! Do you think he'll be happy that we're applying for jobs at the zoo?"

"Probably," Neeka said. "Though I'm not sure working at the zoo's gift shop has much to do with biology."

Standing in the grand hall with their fellow students chatting away beside them, they heard the first warning bell rang.

Payton looked sadly at Neeka. "Guess I better go. Our classes are in opposite directions. I wish we had more time to talk."

"Guess we shouldn't have stopped for those breakfast burritos."

"So worth it!" Payton sang as she turned away to go to gym class.

Neeka hurried to her locker on the first floor. Thankfully, her first class wasn't too far away. That was handy.

As she walked through the halls, she suddenly felt a hand on her shoulder.

"Hey, Neeka," said a voice she didn't recognize. She turned around, surprised to find George standing behind her.

She'd known George since freshman year. She wouldn't exactly call them good friends, but they'd had a few classes together throughout the years through most of which Neeka acted as George's relationship coach as he pursued Payton.

With his dark shaggy hair, which his cousin Rose had revealed to them was actually light brown and dyed so he looked like the next Taylor Lautner, Neeka had always thought George was cute, when his big, obnoxious mouth didn't get in the way. He was a little awkward, but the summer had taken a lot of that awkwardness away. He had always been pretty tall, but he had grown even more. And his voice had certainly changed.

Blushing, Neeka smiled. "Hi, George. Payton's at her gym class..."

He bit his lip. "Come on, Neeka, we both know Payton and I are never going to happen. I was pretty bummed about it last year, but I've moved on since then."

"Who's the lucky girl?" Neeka asked, curious.

"No girl. Just living the single life." George winked. "Unless you have any friends you'd like to hook me up with."

"No chance," Neeka said light-heartedly, though she meant it.

"You taking AP Bio this year?" he asked.

Neeka stopped. "Funny you should mention it. Payton and I were just talking about it."

"So you both are?"

"Are you?"

"Yep. And so is my cousin Rose."

"Payton must be delighted. She and Rose are good friends."

George frowned. "You know what this means?"

"What?"

"If you and Payton get into another big fight like you did freshman year, you and I are stuck together as Biology partners." He winked again and walked away.

As Neeka watched him go, she didn't think being stuck at a table next to George all year was a bad thing at all. In fact, she'd quite enjoy it.

****

"Team Scary Pancake's on a mission," Selina announced as the trio made their way to the cafeteria at lunch.

"You going to narrate everything we do?" Neeka asked.

"If the stars in all those Hollywood documentaries get a narrator, so do I."

Neeka wanted to point out that, technically, Selina didn't have a narrator if she was narrating herself, but she instead decided to play along. "All right, our mission is to find Courtney and Val, who will very likely be sitting together at lunch, and pass on the JV torch."

"Torches," Payton corrected. She wiggled the two torches the girls had made out of sticks from her backyard that were bundled together with twine. Each had gold foil on top to represent flames and glued to the middle was a volleyball. One had Courtney's name on it, the other Val's.

"This is so uncool," Selina moaned, though she hadn't complained when they were gluing the torches together.

"It's a lot more fun than the way Coach Mike told us we'd be leaders." Payton put on a gruff voice, imitating their coach. "Girls, come to my office. You're leaders. Now get out so I can secretly dance to classic rock songs and eat popcorn."

Neeka and Selina laughed at her impression as they entered the cafeteria. Payton came across as quiet sometimes, but she sure could be funny, when she put aside her insecurities.

"I see them over in the corner," Selina said and hurried over, leaving Neeka and Payton to catch up.

It was only as they reached the table that Neeka realized the two girls

64

were surrounded by what seemed like half the sophomore class. *Oh yeah, they're both Miss Popular.*

Val and Courtney were surprised to see them.

"What's up?" Courtney asked.

Selina scooted in beside them, oblivious to the crowd around the girls. "We wanted to eat lunch with you."

Val and Courtney looked at each other and shrugged their shoulders, giving in. "Okay," they said in unison.

"But maybe outside instead, under the willow tree," Neeka suggested, pulling Selina up by the collar of her polo shirt. Standing, Selina scowled. Neeka continued. "We want to discuss a volleyball issue with you."

The girls looked as if this made more sense than the girls simply wanting to eat with them.

"Of course," Val said in her chirpy voice that she put on when she was the center of attention. "Can we meet you there in ten?"

"Perfect," Payton answered before Neeka had a chance to. "I still need to get my lunch. I'm starved."

As Payton left to stand in line, Courtney asked, "Why doesn't she just pack a lunch?"

"Because she would eat it before the morning bell rang," Neeka said. "See ya in ten."

It was more like twenty minutes before the girls met them under the willow tree, leaving Team Scary Pancake less time than they thought to carry out their mission.

"Valerie Sutton and Courtney Adams," Neeka said ceremoniously, causing Payton and Selina to giggle next to her. "We have gathered you here today for a very important reason."

Courtney folded her arms, but she had a smile on her face.

Val looked confused.

"We didn't think it would happen again this year, but because we lost so many seniors last year, Coach Mike is once again putting some girls on both JV and varsity."

"Yes, we know," Val said impatiently, eager for Neeka to get to the point.

"Thank God, it's not us," Selina said, indicating Team Scary Pancake.

"Varsity all the way, baby."

"But you two will be playing for both teams," Neeka said. "And though we do not like the way you singled Payton out last year, there's no denying the other girls on the JV team look to you for support."

"Okay, mom," Courtney joked.

Val looked more regretful.

Neeka elbowed Payton softly in the ribs. "Now."

"Ouch," Payton squeaked, but reached into her bag and pulled out the two torches.

Neeka handed them to the girls. "These are for you. We are officially passing responsibilities for leadership of JV over to you."

As Courtney's eyes lit up, Val's looked down, uncertain. Neeka didn't blame her. She remembered when Coach Mike told her she would be a leader for the first time. It was a lot of responsibility to take on. It was one thing to be popular; it was another to be a leader. Being a leader could be scary at times.

"Since you'll also be on varsity, the new freshman girls in particular will be looking up to you. Whether your realize it or not, the girls will be copying your behavior. You set the tone for practice. You can't mess around like you did last year. You have to make sure everyone feels like part of the team."

Val nodded, quiet while she listened, intent, as if this was the most important thing she'd ever heard.

At least she's taking it seriously, Neeka thought, then she added, "You're helping to shape Hickory Academy's future. One day, all the JV girls will be on varsity. Make sure everyone knows how to approach the drills. Show them what it means to work hard."

"We will," Val promised, gripping her torch tightly. "We'll do everything we can to set the right example at practice."

****

"Do you remember when all the fruit flies escaped?" Neeka asked, setting her books down on one of the back tables in the Biology lab. "There were literally thousands of flies buzzing around our heads."

Payton laughed. "And it was right before Parents' Night."

The Biology lab looked the same as it always did. Instead of desks, the room was crowded with black lab tables. At the front of the room was a demonstration counter and, to the side, Dr. B's desk.

Their Biology teacher, Dr. Ronald Beamon, was currently slouched behind his desk rifling through papers, his reading glasses clipped to his collar. Neeka still didn't understand why a man in his thirties needed reading glasses. His grandpa posture and the grey streaks in his brown hair made him seem a lot older than he actually was. Maybe it was a British thing. Perhaps guys in Britain aged faster.

He really had been a huge help to them over the past two years. They'd often gone to him for advice, more often than to the guidance counselors at the school. He'd become their mentor. Neeka was glad to be back in his class.

At one of the tables in front of them, George sat with his cousin Rose. Knowing Payton well, Rose had greeted them kindly when they'd entered, but George had barely said a word.

Payton followed Neeka's eye line. "I feel really bad," she whispered. "I hope George will at least still consider me a friend."

"Give him time," Neeka said. "He really liked you last year."

"At one point, I thought I might like him too, but he's really not my type. I'm more into athletes."

Neeka sat a little straighter. "So there's definitely no way you'd ever date George? You have absolutely no feelings for him at all?"

Payton shook her head confidently. "Nope."

"And if someone else started dating him, you wouldn't mind?"

"I'll even set them up."

Unable to help herself, Neeka smiled. "Interesting."

Payton leaned back in her chair, looking around. "Sitting at this table again brings back so many memories. Do you remember sitting here freshman year and wondering what the first practice of the school year would be like? We were so nervous! I mean, we'd already met the team at camp at the community center, but there's a different feeling at practice when the school year starts. It means the start of the season is nearly official. I think that's why we were so nervous. We had no idea what to expect from the season. We'd never played volleyball at a competitive level before."

"We're very different players now," Neeka noted.

"You are. Me—not so much."

Neeka was surprised to hear Payton say it. Her friend had acknowledged her growth in the past. Why was she shying away from it now? "But you've come such a long way."

"Improved, yes, but I wouldn't say I'm a star volleyball player just yet."

"You're a starter on varsity. Did you ever think that would happen?"

Payton smiled slightly. "I hoped, but I wasn't fully confident. I mean, I did start at that match last year, but I was still afraid I'd be playing JV this year."

The conversation ended there as Dr. B started class. He welcomed them to a new year and informed them they would be treated like university students. They could go to the bathroom or sharpen their pencils when they wanted to. It was all the same as it had been during Biology their freshman year. With their extra privileges, he would expect them to behave like mature young adults.

As Dr. B began to go over the syllabus for the year, Neeka let her mind drift. She dreamed of playing volleyball in space, then of George taking her to the homecoming dance. At no point last year did she ever think she would have a crush on George, but over the summer, she'd found herself thinking a lot about him. The way he made her laugh... when he wasn't irritating her to the point she wanted to flick his eyebrows. But there was no way she could ask him out. It would be too awkward, after the way he fawned over Payton last year. Plus, she was certain he only thought of her as a friend.

"You really are a space case," Payton said, nudging her friend.

Neeka looked up at her, confused.

"Dr. B just ended class," she explained.

"Oh." Neeka's cheeks felt hot.

To her utter humiliation, Payton noticed. "You thinking about that secret crush of yours?"

"No," Neeka declared, too adamantly.

"Uh huh."

Neeka grabbed her books. "Let's just get out of here."

"I was actually thinking we could talk to Dr. B first. I want to say a proper hello and let him know how volleyball was doing."

Quickly looking to the front of the room to make sure George was gone, Neeka agreed. Talking to Dr. B was always a good idea. As their mentor, he always had something wise to say.

But as they approached his desk, before they could launch into their latest volleyball issues, Neeka immediately noticed a piece of shiny gold metal on Dr. B's ring finger.

"You got married!" she exclaimed.

Dr. B looked up, startled. "Yes," he answered in his soft voice. "Over the summer."

Neeka and Payton had met his girlfriend freshman year. She was stunning. And smart. Neeka was surprised, but thrilled for him. Though one of the toughest teachers in their school, Dr. B was a good man. He deserved to be happy. "Congrats!"

Payton was just as excited for Dr. B. "That's uber cool!"

"Yes, well, thanks," Dr. B said, an unending smile in his eyes. Usually he was so monotone, it was the most emotion she'd ever seen on his face. "And how is volleyball going?"

"We have our first practice today!" Payton spryly informed him. "And I'm starting!"

Full of surprises that day, Dr. B awkwardly pumped his fist into the air and yelled, "Yay! Rah!"

Neeka looked at Payton and did everything she could not to burst out laughing. She didn't want to hurt Dr. B's feelings nor ruin his newfound enthusiasm, but the whole thing was just so unlike their mentor, she couldn't help but feel the giggles coming on. Her lip quivered and she was unable to speak.

Thankfully, Payton was more composed. "We've got to jet to our next class, but we'd like to come talk to you some more tomorrow, during lunch, if that's ok," she asked.

"My door is always open," Dr. B said sincerely.

As soon as the girls were outside the classroom and around the corner, the laughter they'd held in exploded from them. Neeka laughed so hard, her side went sore.

"Now I love Dr. B even more," she confessed.

"Me too!" Payton said. "He is by far my favorite teacher here."

****

As soon as school was finished for the day, the girls ran to the locker rooms to change for practice. When they got there, Selina was already dressed and ready to go, explaining she had gym as her last class of the day. As they entered the locker room one by one, the team chatted eagerly, impatient for the new season to officially begin. Their first match was only a week away.

Over the summer months, after camp had finished, the JV and varsity girls had continued meeting, unofficially, at the community center. Neeka felt it was important they practice several times throughout the week so that they could use their experience at camp to improve their skills, recreating many of the drills Coach Murphy and Coach Hopkins had taught them. They had also continued to work on their jump serves, with Payton leading the way. Neeka could almost do one herself. She had the power, but the height of her jump was a little off. Still, it was progress.

"So this is it," Neeka said, gathering the girls around in the locker room. "Coach Mike is waiting for us out there. Once we step foot out of this locker room, it'll be the start of Hickory Academy's fifth volleyball season. We've come so far in such a short amount of time, but we still have a ways to go. Our goal is to get to State. We need to keep that goal in mind every practice and every match. We can't let it slip away from us. Starting now, I want you all to keep your eye on the prize. I believe in us. I know we all have the potential to win, if we work hard. Let's make history once again for Hickory Academy. Let's bring home the State trophy!"

CHAPTER 8

The zoo gift shop was mayhem. Families from all over were trying to get their last-minute trips in before the school year took over their life. Kids ran around wild among the African safari puzzles and the Arctic animal snow globes. Next to them, a giraffe toy the size of Neeka grinned wildly. Usually, Payton would find a stuffed toy the size of her friend funny. But not today.

"Are we sure about this?" Payton asked, looking at the frazzled staff at the register. "We can still try the smoothie place near our school."

"And have to serve our fellow classmates wearing those ridiculous uniforms?" Neeka said. "I'd rather live in the lion cages. This will be way more fun."

Payton watched as a kid screamed for his mom to buy him a reptarium he had put a toy lizard in.

"Yeah, fun."

Their turn at the register came. Straightening up, Neeka approached the guy with a confident smile. "We'd like to speak to the manager, please."

The guy didn't look impressed, but maybe he was just tired. "She's on her lunch break. Is there anything I can help you with?"

"We want to apply for work."

He reached his hand forward. "If you leave your resumes with me, I'll make sure they get to her."

Neeka eyed him suspiciously, but realizing they had little other choice, Payton took the resumes from her hand and passed them over. "Thanks."

"Yeah, thanks," Neeka echoed reluctantly.

Payton was relieved. She'd secretly been praying for this. She really did want to work at the zoo. It beat stacking smelly shoes at the bowling alley or picking up garbage in the park. But the idea of being interviewed by the manager terrified her.

"I still don't understand how listing our sports achievements will help us get employed," she said as they left the gift shop and wandered over to a pretzel stand.

"It shows we are dedicated and willing to work hard. Since neither of us have any type of work experience, we have to give them some evidence we're up for the job. Oh my stars, look!" Neeka said, pointing toward a woman in a grassy area with a large leather glove covering her arm. "We're in time for the bird show!"

"I still don't understand why you're so obsessed with animals that can fly," Payton said. "Personally, birds creep me out."

"My whole dream is to fly in a spacecraft someday. Of course I'm obsessed with anything to do with flying."

"Yeah, but look at those things flying toward her. They are uuuuugly."

Payton watched as two giant black birds, each bald, landed on the woman's glove.

"Those are black vultures," Neeka told her. "And even though they're ugly, they're actually kind of sweet. They stay together for life."

The fact jostled Payton's memory. "Are you going to tell me who your secret crush is?" she asked. "I don't understand why it's such a big secret."

Neeka looked down, embarrassed. Payton couldn't remember the last time she saw her friend blush.

"It's nothing."

"Renika Leigh, I've known you for a very long time. Tell me. Who do you like?"

Neeka remained quiet, obviously struggling with the information. Finally, she blurted out, "It's George, okay. I have a tiny, mouse-size crush on George."

Payton immediately burst out laughing, much to Neeka's annoyance. She couldn't help it. All this secrecy over George? She couldn't care less that Neeka liked him. In fact, she thought they'd make a great couple. They were both witty, and George was cute. This year more than ever.

"Why are you laughing?" Neeka demanded, the red in her face now more to do with anger than embarrassment.

"Because I don't understand why you felt you had to keep it a secret."

"I think it's totally obvious. He's been in love with you since freshman year."

"Yeah, but not anymore. I can tell. He doesn't look at me the same way he used to."

Neeka shook her head, the anger in her face disappearing. "It doesn't matter. I don't think he's at all interested in me."

"He'd be crazy not to be," Payton said. She felt bad. Despite her resistance, it was clear Neeka really liked George. She wondered if there was anything she could do to set them up. She really wasn't the matchmaker type, but she'd try to think of something, for Neeka's sake.

"And what about you?" Neeka asked. "Is there anyone you like?"

Payton huffed. "Nope. No unless you count the entire US swim team. Anyway, I don't really have time for boys right now. Until the season is over, I just want to concentrate on volleyball."

"You still worried about what Coach Murphy said regarding putting more emotion into your game?"

"I know I have the passion inside me for volleyball, I wouldn't have stuck with it if I didn't, but knowing it's there doesn't help. I have to find a way to let it out when I'm playing. I thought I was nearly there by the end of camp, but I haven't been able to play that way since we left."

Neeka considered this. "Why don't you ask your dad? He's been your coach for all things sports-related since you were little. He's seen you put intensity into how you play basketball and tennis and all other sports you excel at. Maybe he'll be able to tell you what you're doing differently in volleyball."

"Yeah, my dad probably is the best person to take this to. It's just hard with him living in Cincinnati." She picked at her pretzel, feeling a sudden surge of emotion, wishing her dad was living back in Nashville. "I can't show him what I'm talking about if he's not here."

"Just call him," Neeka insisted. "You've always turned to him in the past. Don't stop now."

****

"I'm glad you called me, baby girl," Brandon Moore said over the phone after Payton finished telling him about camp and Coach Murphy. "You know I'm always here to help."

"So what do you think?" Payton asked. "I see the drive and passion the other girls play with, especially Neeka. But for whatever reason, I can't match it."

"I know you have it in you, pumpkin. I wonder what's holding you back. Are you still feeling insecure about your skills? Because you've come so far—"

"No," Payton said, cutting him off though she appreciated his encouragement. "I mean, yes, I have my bouts of insecurity, but I'm more determined this year than any other to continue my improvement. It's not my lack of skills holding me back."

Brandon went quiet, thinking.

"It's just so frustrating," Payton continued after a moment. "By the end of camp, I could really feel my emotions coming out as I played, almost like I was dancing to my own determination, especially knowing those other girls thought we were all rich private school girls who paid our way through the championships. I was so angry. But now—nothing."

"Payton, you are a fighter. There is no denying that. Growing up, you could be quite shy at times. I've often thought athletics to be your voice, your way of showing the world the power you have inside you. At camp, Hickory Academy was the underdog. The other teams underestimated you. You had to fight for the respect you deserved. When you're among your team at practice, you don't have to prove yourself. They've seen how hard you've worked over the years. Is there any way to simulate the camp experience? Anywhere you can go to feel that outside pressure again? Before the season starts."

"You mean find strangers to play with?"

"Bingo."

"Yeah, I guess there's a few places I could try."

"Then do it, baby girl. Go out and show Nashville all you've got."

****

"Mom, I'm heading to the fitness center," Payton announced, shouting near the front door, her bag in hand.

Her mom appeared from the kitchen wearing her purple cleaning gloves. "You've only just finished dinner. What's the rush?"

"I want to practice my volleyball skills."

Her mom frowned. "I find that rather odd. You had volleyball practice today after school. Aren't you sick of volleyball practice?"

"Mom, please. Not now. This is important. The fitness center is only down the street."

"But you haven't been there in years. Not since—"

"Dad moved out. I know. Listen, I promise I'm not meeting a boy or anything like that. I just want to practice."

Alison studied her then threw her soapy gloves into the air. "Fine. As long as your homework is finished, you can go."

"It is. Thanks, Mom." Payton ran over to give her mom a kiss on the cheek before hurrying out the door.

It was still light out, but twilight would come soon enough. She wanted to be back before it was dark. She hated being alone on the streets in the dark. It scared her. Her plan was to go in, check out the volleyball courts, maybe play a few sets, then head home.

The fitness center was small, but it was up to date on all the latest facilities. A lot of families from the neighboring estates used the fitness center, preferring the sense of community within it over the larger gyms around the city.

As Payton entered the building, an older woman with a bright smile greeted her at the reception desk.

"Payton Moore! Oh my, we haven't seen you in years. Child, you have grown so much!"

Payton smiled. Dorothy had been the receptionist here for as long as she could remember. She suddenly felt bad for not visiting over the last few years. "Hi, Dorothy. Is my dad's account still active?"

Dorothy did a quick check on the computer. "It sure is. I'll have a new membership card mailed out to you, in case it's my day off the next time you come in. It sure is great to see you."

"You too, Dorothy." Payton waved goodbye as she headed toward the female locker room.

Once she was dressed, wearing her volleyball shorts and a Titans T-shirt, she made her way toward the gym, happy when she spotted a group of guys playing a three-on-three volleyball match on the left half of the gym. The reason she'd chosen the fitness center was because she remembered watching people setting up volleyball nets when she used to come here to have her dad coach her before the basketball season. It was a volleyball hot-spot.

Payton watched the guys play. They were a little older than her, probably in their early twenties. The clear leader among them was a guy with blue eyes so dark they were almost black. They all shouted banter at one another, but Blue Eyes was the loudest, using the banter to encourage his friends to play better.

They are kind of a mess, Payton thought, though she felt bad doing so, remembering the days when she could barely hit a ball.

It didn't appear they had any formal training. Passing with one arm, they shanked passes all over the court, leaving little time to prepare for their next move. When they spiked the ball, their arms swung wildly, taking away from their precision. Instead of setting up plays, they immediately hurried to send the ball over the net.

But they did have an inner fire. Payton could see it written clearly on their faces and in the way they bantered. Their lack of skills had nothing to do with a lack of effort, will, or determination.

Her dad's words came back to her. *When you're among your team at practice, you don't have to prove yourself.*

Obviously, these guys were trying to prove themselves to each other. The heat was on, and they were stepping up full force.

Payton lingered on the sidelines, continuing to watch them play, trying to get the courage to ask if she could join. This was just what she needed. She needed to learn how to play with the same frantic, fast-paced energy.

Unless it causes me to be reckless, she suddenly thought, wondering if playing with such intensity would cause her to lose control. Then she shook the thought away. *No, I have plenty of control. It can only take me so far. I need to step up my game. This is how.*

Steeling herself, she finally stepped forward onto the court. "Can I play?" she asked, but the guys, intent on their game, didn't hear her.

Taking a deep breath, she tried again. "Can I play?" she shouted, trying to make her voice as loud as Coach Murphy's.

This caught the attention of Blue Eyes, who turned to look at her, just as the ball came flying his way. It bonked him on the head.

"Pause button," he shouted, irritated. "What do you want, kid?" he asked.

"To play," she answered, trying to sound more confident than she felt, something she had grown good at.

"No," Blue Eyes said harshly.

"Why, cuz I'm a girl?" she challenged.

He threw the volleyball casually into the air. "Cuz we already have enough players," he said, his voice sharp.

One of the other guys stepped forward. "Actually, David, I need to take a break. My ankle is still recovering from my fall off the surf board last week. I could use a few minutes to rest."

So the jerk is named David, Payton noted.

"Good thing I'm here then," she said defiantly, trying to bring her inner fire forward, though she felt slightly ridiculous doing so. Part of her wanted to run back to the locker rooms.

"Fine, new girl," David agreed without bothering to ask her name. "I hope you can keep up."

Payton took her spot on the opposite side of the court.

Time to prove myself, she thought as the ball was served.

From the start, it was clear her style of playing was much more organized than the guys'. Studying the ball, she waited patiently in her ready position as it made its way over the net, while the other two guys on her team ran around like chickens, unsure of where it was heading. At one point, one of them knocked her over as he jumped up to strike the ball.

"It was mine!" she protested.

"You were too slow," he said without remorse.

"I thought we were on the same team," she mumbled, helping herself back up.

David prepared to serve. "Too weak to take what you want?" he hollered from the other side. "You might as well give up now, little girl."

Payton glared at him. "Nice one, ogre. What kind of coward picks on the new girl?"

"This ain't high school, darlin'. If you can't handle the heat, get out of the kitchen."

Without answering, Payton steadied herself. When her chance to hit the ball came, she immediately struck it toward David, hoping it would break his toes.

It landed on the ground near him, but instead of earning his respect, the point seemed to egg him on. "Not a bad shot, for a robot," he said. "When your parents ordered you off the assembly line, they should have chosen one with a bit of personality."

She'd experienced this type of harassment before in basketball. Guys didn't handle it well when a girl, especially a younger one, played better than them.

"Don't act so jealous," she countered. "You'll get there someday."

They continued to play. Though David persistently heckled her, he began to smile more. He was obviously impressed that she was sticking around, despite the harshness of his words. She could almost see a gleam of friendship building in his dark blue eyes.

Boys, I'll never understand them, she muttered inwardly.

It wasn't long before she realized she was enjoying herself. It felt good being the best on the court, despite the trash talk the boys threw her way. But more than that, there was a sense of freedom playing with them.

There was no coach or crowds of people judging her every move. She wasn't letting down her teammates if she missed a shot. When she punched the ball over the net, she felt as if she were flying. She felt no need to impress these guys, only a need to cream them.

She probably could have played all night, but when she glanced out the high windows of the gym and saw the sun going down, she knew her time was up. She had to leave.

"I gotta go," she said after scoring what felt like her hundredth point.

She thought David would be pleased, but a flash of disappointment crossed his face. "Can't take it anymore?" he insinuated.

Payton rolled her eyes. "You wish," she shouted behind her as she left.

CHAPTER 9

"JV are killing it!" Selina excitedly said to Payton as they sat in their seats on the bench of the Viking's gymnasium to watch the younger girls play.

An away game, it was their first match of the season. Selina was right; JV was performing like superstars, particularly Val and Courtney. Last year, Hickory Academy JV were the worst in the district. One match in, and this year already looked like it'd be the exact opposite.

A team can change a lot in one year, Payton thought, though the realization brought her little comfort. Like the rest of the varsity girls who sat nervously around her as the supported the JV girls, all she could think about was how, last year, Hickory Academy varsity was undefeated during the regular season and how, this year, they'd be expected to do the same. It was a lot of pressure.

"You worried if varsity will win too?" Neeka asked, reading her well.

Payton decided to be honest, hoping Neeka wouldn't take it the wrong way. "I almost hope we don't. Not the first game, anyway. Then the pressure will be off."

"Don't think that way!" Neeka snapped. "If we're going to get to State, we have to challenge ourselves every chance we get."

And she took it the wrong way. Payton was slightly taken aback. Neeka was stressed when it came to volleyball, but Payton hadn't seen her this defensive since they started playing freshman year.

"I know, Neeka. I'm not giving up before it starts. I was just talking out loud."

Neeka relaxed. "Sorry, I guess the pressure is getting to me too."

Suddenly, the crowd cheered as Val rolled on the ground to dig a ball that was near impossible to save. With the crowd on their feet, Courtney used the energy in the room to pound the ball over for a point.

Payton watched as the JV girls immediately met for a quick huddle, like they did with every point scored. She couldn't hear what they were saying, but it seemed Val and Courtney were doing most of the talking. They were taking their leadership roles seriously. That was good. It set a good example for the other girls.

"The Vikings aren't going to be too happy if they lose on their home turf," Selina predicted. "They may have home court advantage, but we have the Team Scary Pancake advantage. And the Little Pancakes."

"Val and Courtney will never agree to you calling them Little Pancakes," Neeka said. "They're too cool for that."

"In my book, cool equals boring." Selina rubbed her hands together. "I just want to get out there and play."

"Me too," Payton and Neeka said at the same time, then laughed.

Payton stretched. "I doubt the Viking varsity team is as good as they used to be, now that Brianna Jones has graduated. She was a phenomenal server. She never mastered the topspin jump serve, not like I did, but she had a fantastic float serve."

"All the more reason why it was good we spent most of the summer making sure all the girls on varsity learned to jump serve," Neeka said. "We still need work, but at least we can get the ball over the net most of the time. A team full of jump servers gives us a really big advantage."

Payton felt a flicker of her old insecurity pass through her, but she quickly let it go. Being the only girl in the district who could perform a topspin jump serve had been her claim to fame, and one of the main reasons Coach Mike kept her on varsity when it was clear her other skills needed work. Now that most of the Hickory Academy team could do one, her skill was no longer unique. But she didn't mind as much as she thought she would. If summer camp had done anything, it was show how much all the players on the team had to up their game.

At least I still have the best jump serve, Payton thought. Selina wasn't too far behind, and a few of the other girls, including Neeka, were pretty decent, but Payton was a year ahead of them. Her serve had a deadly accuracy to it.

JV finished the game easily, taking home the win.

"We're next," Neeka said, jumping up from her seat. "And so it begins."

****

"Here's to another undefeated season!" Courtney cheered as the volleyball team held up their glasses.

"She seems to forget she wasn't on varsity last year," Selina hissed toward Payton.

As tradition, they celebrated their first match of the season at their local pizza place, a small but colorful restaurant in the heart of downtown Nashville. As Payton held up her glass to toast both JV and varsity's win that evening, it took all her control not to grab a slice of pizza in each hand and chow down.

Ignoring Courtney's speech, Selina reached for the first slice on the pan. Immediately, Payton put her glass down and joined in. The minute the gooey cheese touched her lips, she began to relax.

"Someone's gone to heaven," she heard someone snicker as she closed her eyes, but she didn't know who and she didn't care.

The chatter immediately moved away from the game and onto other exciting topics.

"I'm up for homecoming court," Val announced to everyone.

"I thought only seniors could be homecoming queen," Janette said. "That's the way it was at my school in Memphis."

"Here too, but anyone can be a part of the court. I'd be the Hickory Duchess," Val explained. "It's the top spot for sophomores. A junior is the princess, and a senior the queen. Best of all, Stephen is up to be my escort!"

Giving her crust to Payton, Selina huffed. "Why would you put yourself up for something as superficial and demeaning as choosing who is the prettiest girl in the school? It makes me sick."

Val was indignant. "I'm not getting in on my looks alone. I'm actually nice to people. You should try it sometime."

Selina smiled a sickly sweet smile. "OMG, y'all look so amazing in those gowns," she said, imitating the chirpy voice Val used when she was surrounded by people. It was scarily accurate.

Then she dropped her voice down to its normal level. "See, I can be fake too. I like you better when you're on the court, Sutton. When you're leering at the other side—I think that's when you're truly being yourself."

"I resent that!" Val said, infuriated.

Selina looked genuinely confused. "I meant it as a compliment."

Reaching for her third slice of pizza, Payton suddenly felt a jab in her ribs. "Do you think this is weird?" Neeka whispered.

"Val and Selina going at it? Not at all," Payton said.

"No, the fact that no one is talking about the game. Shouldn't we be going over what we did well and our missteps?"

Payton took a bite of her pizza. Talking with her mouthful, she said, "There is a time to work and there is a time to play. And by play, I mean eat. This is a time to eat."

"Wise words, Yoda, but I'm serious. We should discuss it now, while the match is still fresh on our minds."

Payton scratched her head, thinking. The tough love side of Neeka was emerging again. In a way, she was glad. Neeka had been so practical, not wanting to get their hopes up about winning State. It was nice to see she was finally keeping the dream alive, but now Payton was slightly worried she'd created a monster. Neeka needed to relax and enjoy herself. Years of leading championship basketball teams had taught Payton that there had to be a balance. Neeka was the best volleyball player they had, but she was still new to the whole leadership in sports thing.

Yet... Payton did want to win State really, really, really badly.

"I just don't get why everyone is so subdued about winning," Neeka added. "This is the start of the season. It's time we went into beast mode."

"We're in bestie mode right now," Payton joked, trying to alleviate Neeka's seriousness. It didn't work.

Before Payton could give a further response, Neeka made her decision. She stood up to get everyone's attention. Their booth and the one next to them immediately went quiet. Neeka had that effect on the team. Coach Mike was off somewhere, probably playing an arcade game, but Coach Gina looked up with a curious smile.

"First, I just want to congratulate everyone on our first wins tonight," Neeka began. "It was a fantastic way to start the season. But I think it's important that we remember we still have a long way to go. I'm not trying to be negative; I just want us to prepare for the battle that's ahead. We performed well tonight, had the crowd on their feet, but in the coming practices, we'll need to work on our mistakes. State is our goal. Until we reach it, we can't take anything for granted."

She took a breath then continued. "We have spent a good portion of our lives walking down the halls of Hickory Academy. Some of the best memories of our life have, and will be, during these school years. When I graduate, I want to do something epic. And I want to do it with all of you girls sitting here. Let's bring home Hickory Academy's first State volleyball trophy this year. Let's leave behind the ultimate legacy!"

Payton was amazed. Neeka spoke with such poise and conviction, she could have been mistaken for royalty. She had never witnessed Neeka emit so much charisma and authority before. Neeka's words were so motivational, Payton suddenly had an urge to throw her slice of pizza down and head to the gym to practice, then and there. Around her, the other girls remained silent, surprised but inspired. Taking it all in, it took a few seconds before they applauded.

"We won't let you down," Val promised, all talk of homecoming court vanishing.

"We'll make you proud," Courtney added.

She really is a leader, in the truest form, Payton realized. *All our years as friends, I was always the All-Star. But this entire time, there was another leader sitting by my side.*

CHAPTER 10

"Please, please, please, please, please," Payton said over the phone.

Neeka plopped down on her yellow comforter, staring at the stars stuck to her ceiling. Once again, Payton was begging her to go to the fitness center near her house. It wasn't an ideal way to spend a Sunday. Between homework and volleyball practice, Neeka had been looking forward to some down time. But she knew Payton really wanted her to go, and she wanted to do all she could to make sure Hickory Academy made it to State.

"I really need the help with my hitting drills," Payton pushed.

"Fine, but only so you'll stop pestering me," she said light-heartedly.

"I know you're only half-joking, but I'll take it," Payton said gleefully. "You can park at my house, and we can walk down."

They agreed to meet in an hour and hung up. Perhaps it was a good thing. With both her parents at work and Jamari gone, the house was so empty, it was almost creepy. She missed the sound of Jamari's computer games in the background. Even his obnoxious basketball friends who came to visit.

After stuffing her volleyball gear into her equipment bag, she pulled out her phone and texted him.

I miss you, bean head.

Jumping into the jeep made her feel better. It was fun driving, though a bit scary at times. She was constantly afraid of people jumping out in the middle of the street.

Soon enough, she pulled into Payton's driveway, and Payton was already outside waiting for her, an excited smile on her face.

"I don't think I've seen you this revved up for volleyball... well, ever. There a hot guy at the gym or something?"

She was joking, but the immediate uneasiness that took over Payton told her she'd hit the mark. "Oh my God, who is he?" Neeka asked.

Payton scrunched her eyebrows together, conflicted with emotion. "A jerk, that's who he is. He's so annoying. His good looks are wasted on him, as my mom would say."

Neeka held her hands up. "All right. No more guy talk. Ready?"

Bags in hand, they walked the short distance to the fitness center. Payton was eager to practice, but there was no hurry, so they took their time, enjoying the Sunday afternoon.

"Have you heard back from the zoo yet?" Payton asked.

Neeka's heart instantly began to race. "No, have you?" she asked, wondering if perhaps Payton had scored an interview before her.

"No, not yet. Perhaps it was silly thinking we'd both be hired. If one of us gets it and the other doesn't, let's not be mad, okay?"

"You sure you didn't get a call?" Neeka asked.

"No, I haven't," Payton confirmed, and years of friendship told Neeka she was telling the truth.

"Of course we won't be mad," she confirmed, though she couldn't help thinking how much more she needed the job than Payton did. Payton's mother only wanted to teach her about responsibility, but Neeka actually needed the money. Her parents were very frank about the fact that she would have to put money toward gas and car insurance. "But if we don't hear back soon, either way, I just might have to apply for the smoothie place," she added reluctantly.

"Let's make that plan Z," Payton said. "Maybe when we're finished at the fitness center, we can think of some other places we'd like to work."

"Good idea," Neeka agreed.

When they reached the fitness center, they were greeted by a friendly old lady who instantly recognized Payton, shooing her away when she tried to scan her membership card. They quickly changed into their volleyball clothes then headed for the gym.

Half of the gym was already occupied by six guys playing a three-on-three match. *Did they have jelly for arms?* she thought as she watched them loosely pass the ball. They were clearly having fun, but their game was way off.

As Payton walked across the empty half of the gym to grab a volleyball from the ball stand, the guys instantly turned their attention on her.

"Too scared to face us today?" a blonde guy yelled.

"In your dreams," Payton hollered back as she grabbed a ball. "I'm just sick of always kicking your behinds."

"I think you're all talk and no action," a guy with dark blue eyes said.

"And I think you're all brawn and no brains," Payton fired back.

The guy flexed his muscles. "You've got the brawn part right."

Neeka was surprised. Payton was usually only that open with people she knew well. "Who's Mr. Muscles?" Neeka asked as she met Payton on the court.

"His name is David Span," Payton said. "He's the jerk."

Neeka smiled knowingly. "He is cute."

"And intolerable. I'd rather kiss your Memaw's dentures then go anywhere near him."

"So you have thought about dating him," Neeka teased.

In reply, Payton set the ball high in the air then punched it against the gym wall, causing a loud thump to echo across the open space.

"Watch it, spikey," the guy named David yelled. "I didn't plan on going deaf today."

After setting up the second net, they decided to practice a bump-set-spike drill where Payton passed the ball to Neeka, who set it for Payton, who then spiked it over the net. Payton was doing well, Neeka thought when they were well into the drill. She still lacked the intensity Selina and Courtney had, but her accuracy had improved drastically since the previous year.

"Treat it like a jump serve," Neeka instructed. "Hit with the same force. Just like you did earlier against the gym wall."

"It's difficult," Payton admitted. "When I serve, I'm in complete control of the ball. But when you or anyone else sets the ball for me, I'm too focused on where I'm sending the ball then how I'm sending it."

Neeka stopped the drill, giving her and Payton time to think about how she could do better.

"Your friend give up on you already?" David yelled, causing the other guys to laugh.

Without responding, Payton grabbed the ball from the floor and started the drill again. Neeka couldn't help but notice a new anger fueling Payton's performance. She started sweating harder, and hitting harder.

Interesting, Neeka thought, looking over at the guys.

On the next round, instead of setting to Payton, she held onto the ball. Payton gave her a curious look as Neeka turned around and whistled for the guys' attention.

"You Neanderthals mind if we join you, or are you too worried you'll catch our girl germs?"

David spread his arms out wide. "Bring it on, little darlin'. I'm happy to send you home crying."

"And I'm happy to crush you so hard, you'll have no tears left to cry."

"Nice one," Payton said. "Where did that come from?"

"I have an older brother," Neeka reminded her.

"We don't have to do this," Payton whispered as they moved toward the other half of the gym to join the guys. "I mean, we'll beat them without question. But we don't have to actually play them if you don't want to. They can be pretty brutal with their banter."

"I'll survive. Plus, it'll give me a chance to practice my jump serve," Neeka reassured her. "I keep freezing up at our matches. My desire to send the ball flying into David's pretty face might help."

They switched the game for a four-on-four match with David choosing to be on the opposite side of the net.

Bad decision going against us, Neeka thought as Payton served the first ball. It was too quick for the boys to block. Payton served a few more times before "accidentally" hitting the ball into the net. Neeka suspected she did it to allow the guys to save a little face.

As predicted, the girls dominated the court, even when Payton went easy. They were undoubtedly superior, probably because they were used to setting and hitting properly.

The match turned out to be a lot of fun. And useful. Neeka was particularly proud of her jump serve. It wasn't as mighty as Payton's, but it was getting there. She wasn't as nervous performing it as she usually was. Perhaps wanting to pound the boys to the floor had something to do with that.

As the match approached its end, it was clear the boys were impressed. Even David had little to say as the girls reached the match point during the final set.

"We win," Payton sang happily.

"Only cuz we let you," David countered. "We were tired of looking at each other. We wanted some cute faces to join."

Unable to answer, Payton blushed. To save grace, Neeka immediately pulled her away toward the sidelines where their water bottles waited.

"We should invite David to our games," she teased. "I've never seen you play with so much authority. You were totally present."

"Don't you dare, jelly bean!" Payton warned. "We don't need the likes of him shouting abuse from the bleachers."

"He's only pulling your pig tails," Neeka insisted. "He likes you."

"There are so many things wrong with that statement, I don't know where to begin."

"Like what?" Neeka challenged.

""Besides the fact that he's a jerk, he's twenty-three, way too old for me."

"Oh," Neeka said. She knew he was older, but she didn't realize by so much. "But you can't deny you perform much better when he's around. He's the magic bean you've been missing all this time."

"Beans give you indigestion," Payton objected.

"But you still eat them. So with all the cons aside, how do you really feel about him? Is it love or hate?"

"Both," Payton admitted quietly.

"Ha, that was a trick question," Neeka said. "The opposite of love isn't hate. It's indifference. Love and hate are nearly the same thing."

Payton took a sip from her bottle. "I've been playing with them now and again over the last few weeks. The boy irritates the hot dogs out of me, but there's something about him..."

"That's all I need to hear," Neeka said. Knowing what she had to do to help Payton, she turned to the guys. "I don't know if Payton has told you, but we go to Hickory Academy. You all can feel free to stop by our games anytime. See what great volleyball looks like."

Payton glared at her. "I hate you."

Neeka put her arm around her friend. "Which means you love me."

CHAPTER 11

"Demonbreun High."

The name of Hickory Academy's archrivals rolled off Neeka's tongue like hot lava. The girls of Demonbreun High were used to being on top, but Hickory Academy had knocked them off their throne two years ago. Since then, the Demonbreun girls had made it their primary mission to settle the score.

The match was a home game, but the bleachers were full of black and yellow-coated fans, the Demonbreun High colors. It was a highly anticipated match. If anyone was going to destroy Hickory Academy's undefeated winning streak, it was going to be these girls.

"I heard they brought in a celebrity coach over the summer to help them with their overall skills, including their jump serves," Janette said, peeking out of the locker room door behind Neeka.

"I doubt that," Neeka said.

Janette didn't look so sure. "I guess we're about to find out. For once, I don't think I mind being the sub."

The Demonbreun girls glared at the Hickory Academy fans, fueling their determination. Neeka couldn't help but feel like she had freshman year when she faced Demonbreun for the first time on the JV team, before Hickory Academy had started making a name for itself. They had been so intimidating. They were the measuring stick against which all the other teams in the district compared themselves, and at the time, Hickory

Academy could barely keep up.

"Now we're the measuring stick," she said out loud.

Payton came up behind them. "Time for our team meeting." She strained her neck. "Our dads here yet?"

"Yeah," Neeka said, pointing to the top of the bleachers. "They both made it in time."

Just then, a huge cry broke out among the juniors and seniors behind them in the locker room.

"Annette!" one of the girls cried.

Neeka, Janette, and Payton looked at each other. No way! There was no way Annette was here. On instinct, Neeka felt herself tense up.

Hurriedly, they joined the rest of their team, who had formed a semi-circle around none other than Annette Reynolds.

"What is she doing here?" Selina hissed behind them.

Annette had been their captain when they were freshmen. The girl was ruthless. She'd used intimidation to try to get the girls to perform better, but it had backfired. They'd lost all sense of teammanship and started playing for themselves instead of for each other. As a result, they'd started performing poorly, coming back only at the end of the season when the excitement of Payton's jump serve had bonded them as a team.

Neeka didn't hate Annette, but she certainly didn't want Annette's bad influence to rub off on the team. She attributed most of Hickory Academy's success to the fact that varsity, and now JV, had formed what felt like a sisterhood.

But as Neeka stepped closer, she noticed something different about Annette. The brunette waves of her hair were a lot longer than they used to be, and the hard lines that used to accompany her scowl had gone away. Her brown eyes were softer, more friendly and open.

College has changed her, Neeka noted.

Spotting the girls in the back, Annette gave a wide smile. "Well, there's the champs," she said and opened her arms out, inviting them in for a hug.

Awkwardly, the juniors stepped forward and embraced their former captain in a group hug. As they did, Selina opened her mouth to make what would likely be a smart remark, but Neeka quickly stepped on her toe to shut her up.

Most of the girls around them watched on with blank faces, unsure of who stood before them. Thankfully, Coach Mike made the introduction as the girls broke away from their hug.

"For those who didn't have the privilege, Annette was a key player on Hickory Academy's very first volleyball team five seasons ago. Under her leadership, we brought home our very first District and Regional championship trophies her senior year when she was captain."

Neeka could physically sense Selina trying to hold her tongue.

She wasn't much of a leader, Neeka agreed silently, but it was hard to hold a grudge when a much happier, more mature Annette stood in front of them.

Annette accepted Coach Mike's words with modesty. "You were the brains behind the operation, Coach. I just did as I was told."

"Why don't you say a few words?" he encouraged her, clearly delighted one of his prodigies was back. Neeka had to admit, Annette had been a killer *libero*.

"Demonbreun has always been Hickory Academy's biggest rival. That is unlikely to change anytime soon," she began. "The teams you meet at Sub-State and beyond, you only see once and for a very short time. Demonbreun will always be your neighbors. Not only do you meet them several times throughout the year, but you also eat at the same restaurants as them, go to the same movie theaters, and sit next to them at the same concerts. They're inescapable."

"Is this supposed to help?" Selina whispered.

"That makes Demonbreun High your greatest asset," Annette proclaimed. "They will always be there to challenge you, to push you harder. And, whether you realize it or not, you do the same for them. Don't be intimidated by them. Think of them as the team that is going to make you worthy of State, the team that is going to make you work hard enough that you beat them and everyone else who stands between you and the State trophy."

She turned and stared directly at Neeka, Payton, and Selina. "I'm so proud of you girls, of the level you've brought Hickory Academy to. I've been keeping tabs on you while at college, and I can't wait to see you play tonight."

Zowzers, Neeka thought. *Where was this Annette two years ago?*

****

Demonbreun High had obviously prepared for this match. Neeka could see it in their confidence as the two teams slapped hands under the net before the start of the match. They were almost gloating, as if they had a secret no one else knew.

But it was Hickory Academy who had the secret.

It didn't matter how hard Demonbreun High had trained or how much homework they had done. Demonbreun was prepared to go against a team as good as Hickory Academy was last year. They hadn't seen Hickory Academy post camp at Jackson University.

As predicted, any smugness Demonbreun carried disappeared the instant Selina served. They'd known Payton had a jump serve, but they weren't ready when Selina hammered the ball straight to the floor beneath their feet—an ace.

It took a while, with Selina pounding out one serve after the next, but Demonbreun eventually claimed the ball for themselves. As a girl with long red hair waited to serve, Neeka watched as the girl's teammates recomposed themselves. To the surprise of Hickory Academy, the redhead had a perfect float serve, one Val was unable to dig.

Someone's been practicing. Neeka wondered if all of Demonbreun's volleyball team could now jump serve, like most of Hickory Academy could. If so, they could be in trouble.

The redhead scored another three points before the ball returned to Hickory Academy.

Next to serve was Courtney, who was Selina's equal when it came to putting a topspin on the ball. Neither of them were quite as good as Payton, but they were getting pretty close.

Demonbreun had a hard time reaching the ball, but they managed to dig it out. However, it had clearly disrupted any plan of attack they might have had. Their *libero* sent the ball flying into the air in no particular direction. A back row hitter had to pass it to the front row, bypassing their setter completely. With no opportunity to strike, their middle hitter simply passed the ball back over the net to Hickory Academy.

There was no need for Val to lunge for it. Neeka was able to track the ball easily and set it toward their own hitters, allowing Payton to put it away for a point.

As the first set continued, it became very clear very fast that Demonbreun struggled with Hickory Academy's jump serve. Their rivals had also improved over the summer, but not enough to keep up. It seemed the redhead was the only one on their team with a comparable serve. They had thought she would make them Hickory Academy's equal, Neeka assumed, but it didn't.

Hickory Academy won the first set with very little effort.

Neeka looked up into the stands where her papa and Mr. Moore were on their feet, cheering.

She waved up at them then joined her team as they prepared for the next set. Across the court, the Demonbreun girls didn't look as confident as they had at the start of the match, but they also weren't beaten by any means. They were solemn but determined, completely focused as the coach went over a few notes with them.

The redhead caught Neeka staring at them. She smiled, but Neeka couldn't interpret the meaning behind it, not until the girl lifted her arm straight out and turned her thumb downward.

"Looks like someone is trying to warn us," Selina said behind her, then she mouthed, "Fat chance," at the girl.

Neeka thought of the notes she'd seen Coach Mike write when they were at camp watching the scrimmage between Bridgewater and Templeton, the powerhouses.

"They have no intention of losing," Neeka said. "Never underestimate an underdog."

"Did someone say hot dog?" Payton asked, joining them on the court.

Neeka didn't have time to answer. The ref blew her whistle, signally for the players to take their positions.

Forty-five minutes later, Selina threw daggers at Neeka as they rotated. "I blame you for this," she accused. "You and your underdog speech."

Neeka glanced up at the scoreboard. Going into the fifth set, they were tied 2-2. Whoever won this set took home the game.

"Focus!" Neeka shouted at her teammates. "There's no reason we shouldn't win this match!"

It was true. Demonbreun High hadn't suddenly improved after the first set. They had simply played harder. When Hickory Academy served, they dug deep for the ball, crashing to their knees. Their pure will was their defense.

It had unsettled Hickory Academy. Their serves were no longer effective in scoring them points. They had to rely on their hitters, who were all having trouble getting the ball past Demonbreun's grit. They didn't know what to do to score. Long rally after long rally had ensued.

The tension from the spectators in the stands was palpable. They were eerily quiet, not sure what to make of what was happening before them. Hickory Academy was clearly the stronger team, but somehow Demonbreun was not allowing them an edge.

"Keep it loose. Don't get timid on me now, ladies!" Coach Mike barked from the bench. "You've worked hard all summer. Show these girls what you're made of!"

But the damage had been done. Knowing they were at risk of losing, Neeka watched helplessly as her teammates lost their focus, making one mental error after another. Val couldn't always reach the ball. Passes were off. Payton tried to put emotion into her game, but at the cost of her timing. She kept getting blocked. Even Selina was hitting the ball into the net, her face wrought with frustration.

As Demonbreun scored the winning point of the match, the redhead smirked her way. "Told you so," she mouthed, delighted.

Neeka couldn't believe it. Fuming, she watched as their rivals danced around the court like they'd just won the freak'n District Championship. How could Hickory Academy make so many mistakes?

She looked up at the bleachers to where Annette was sitting. Chatting happily with friends beside her, she didn't seem to mind at all that Hickory Academy had just lost.

Well, I do, Neeka thought angrily. *We're the better team. There was no reason we should have lost tonight.*

Maybe Annette had been on to something with her no tolerance policy. As soon as they made it back to the locker room, Neeka let the girls have it. "Where were you girls tonight, out in la la land? Your minds certainly weren't in the game. We should have won."

"We knew we couldn't be undefeated forever," Selina argued.

"I'm not worried about whether we're undefeated. Demonbreun High is nowhere near the same caliber as the teams we'll face at State. We can't take a single game for granted. You weren't trying your best, and that simply isn't good enough. It will never be good enough. What were you thinking?"

"According to you, nothing at all," Selina said angrily, but she was the only one on the defensive.

Around her, the rest of the girls hung their heads low, staring uneasily at the floor.

They can't look at me, Neeka thought. *Good.*

****

Later, after a pep talk from Coach Mike, the girls were given the okay to leave. As her teammates left the locker room, their eyes still glued to the floor, Neeka felt a hand on her shoulder.

"We need to talk, jelly bean," Payton said, looking somber.

"Is this a Team Scary Pancake meeting?" Neeka asked, thankful her friends felt the same way she did. They needed to discuss the team's mistakes.

"Of sorts," Payton said, leading her out into the near-empty gymnasium.

"Aren't we supposed to meet our dads for dinner?" Neeka asked, wondering why they couldn't talk in the locker room. She was looking forward to their daddy-daughter dinner. She didn't want to be late.

"We're going to meet them at the restaurant in a little while."

Payton was being awfully serious. Neeka began to suspect this was more than a simple Team Scary Pancake meeting.

Her fears were proved correct when they caught up to Selina in the privacy of the equipment room.

"Who died and made you the Evil Queen?" Selina ranted the moment she saw Neeka. "What, did Annette swap bodies with you or something?"

Neeka instantly put up her guard. "It's called tough love."

"It's called being a jerk," Selina said. "And that's the nicest word I can use."

"You were kind of harsh," Payton agreed, but she looked uncomfortable saying it.

Neeka couldn't believe it. Could no one else see how badly they'd played tonight? It was not something they could simply shrug off.

"It's not like you can talk," Neeka snapped. "You were the worst out there."

Payton looked hurt by the comment, but Selina was nothing short of infuriated.

"And you think you're Miss Perfect?" she screamed. "Get over yourself, hot shot. You have the easiest job out there. You don't have to dive for the ball like Val does or simultaneously block and hit the ball, the way the hitters do. You're a great setter, but that's only because you can't do anything else."

Payton quickly stepped in between the girls. It was a good thing. Neeka was one insult away from shoving Selina into the ball stand. "We had a bad game. It happens," Payton said, then focused on Neeka. "I don't think you realize how much the other girls look up to you, more than anyone else. They take everything you say to heart. After you spoke to them the way you did tonight, they were gutted. You're their hero. They need you to support them."

Neeka was stunned. She knew the girls looked up to her, but she didn't realize how much. Their hero? She thought that was pushing it, but she relaxed, feeling the tension leave her body, but her mind hadn't changed. They hadn't played their best tonight. She didn't want them to think it was okay, not when they could do better.

"Annette was wrong," Neeka said. "Demonbreun High isn't responsible for pushing us to work harder and play better. We have to do it ourselves. And if you two won't, I will."

****

"Sounds like Selina was putting it nicely when she called you a jerk," Jamari said over the phone.

"Not funny," Neeka said. "Come on, Jamari, this is really important."

"Is it really, sis? It's just one game."

Neeka sat on the cushions next to her bedroom window, suddenly regretting her decision to call her brother. The fact that Selina and Payton had felt the need to confront her stung. They were making her out to be some sort of bully, which she knew she was far from being. She had hoped her brother would give her some guidance, but he was taking their side.

"You're such a hypocrite. You've been captain of nearly every basketball team you've been on, most of which have won championships. I bet you didn't get to that level telling your teammates to stop and smell the roses."

"It isn't black or white, sis. Remember the story I told you last year about the coach that treated us harshly, to the point we reported him to the assistant coach because we weren't having fun? You certainly aren't going to keep the respect of your team if you continue yelling at them. Once you lose their respect, you lose everything."

"I'm not trying to scare them. I just don't want this to be where we start to go downhill. I want us to rise to the top."

"Listen, you're new to this whole leadership thing when it comes to sports, but let me tell you this—your job isn't to win State all on your own. You have to do it as a team. To do so, you have to stay a team. Screaming matches with Selina and picking your teammates apart aren't going to help. Your responsibility as a leader is to keep the team together. That's it. Let Coach Mike do the rest."

"I'm not sure I agree. Coach Mike teaches us the skills we need and he strategizes on how we can use those skills to win, but he can't convince the girls to own up to those skills, not the same way I and the rest of the girls he's chosen as leaders can. That's the whole reason he's trying this new no captain, many leaders thing—so that there are several people out there motivating the girls to play their best."

Jamari sighed, giving in. "You really feel they should have played better?"

"Yes," Neeka said sharply.

"Then do what you believe is best, but keep in mind this is only one loss. You'll have other opportunities to pay Demonbreun High back. Just make sure the team is still united when you do."

CHAPTER 12

It was a stand-off.

Payton watched as from Dr. B's desk as Neeka and Selina faced each other in the Biology lab during lunch. Dr. B stood between them, the acting judge as each side pleaded her case.

It'd taken over a week to get to this point. Selina had grown tired of watching Neeka grind her way through practice, calling everyone out on their mistakes. It'd gotten to the point that the girls tensed up when Neeka was around, causing them to make even more mistakes.

"It's like having Annette around all over again," Selina said. "You're making things worse, Neeka, not better. Lighten up and have a bit of fun."

Payton bit her lip. She sided with Selina. Neeka had gone overboard. But Payton knew it came from a good place. Neeka wanted the girls to win because she knew the girls wanted to win. In her own way, she thought she was doing everyone a favor by forcing them to work harder.

Funny though, Payton thought. *If I'd predicted this exact scene, I would have assumed the sides would be flipped, that it'd be Neeka defending the girls and Selina going all drill sergeant.*

"I'm just being real," Neeka exclaimed. "How else are we going to get to State? Remember Jackson Central at camp, the team who beat Cumberland Lake? Do you think we're ready to beat them yet? We're halfway through the season, and we can't even win against Demonbreun

High!" Selina didn't answer. It was the response Neeka wanted. "No, we're not ready," she continued. "We need to get our act together, to focus and keep pushing ourselves harder."

Payton saw the stress in her friend's eyes. *She's really worried.*

Selina stood her ground. "But the team isn't going to focus if you keep pointing out their faults. They'll just get paranoid that they're doing something wrong. That's a step backward, not forward."

"It's the only way. Last year, we thought we were so great because we went through the entire regular season undefeated. And then we got to Sub-State and learned our skills are nothing compared to the other teams out there. We weren't prepared, because no one pointed out our weaknesses. No one told us we had to be better all-round players. We were strong, but not strong enough. I push the team because I believe in the team. I believe we can get to State. But not as we are now. How we can be if we work harder."

"Well, Hickory Academy doesn't need your type of belief. What's gotten into you, girl?"

"Nothing's gotten into me!" Neeka shouted. "Why can't you see that what I'm doing is right?!"

As the girls continued to go back and forth, Dr. B listened thoughtfully, his head in his hand. Every time one of the girls made a good point, he nodded. Even when they shouted, he didn't quiet them down.

He must be letting them get it out of their system, Payton surmised. It was working. As the argument went on, their voices began to grow softer. They were getting tired arguing the same point over and over again.

"Payton, what do you think?" Dr. B asked when there was a slight break in the debate.

Payton hesitated, not sure how to respond. She didn't want Neeka to feel cornered, but she couldn't side with her either. "I think we need to do what's best for the team."

"That's not an answer," Selina said.

Neeka looked at her expectantly.

Sighing, Payton elaborated. "If we're too relaxed with the girls, there's always the danger they'll slack off, like the younger JV girls did last year.

But we can't be hard on them either. I hate to say it, Neeka, but the girls have been really tense this week. I don't think it's good for their performance or for team spirit for them to be so nervous."

Neeka looked away, disgusted.

Dr. B set his hands on the desk. "Okay, I think I've heard enough. You ladies came here to ask my opinion. That's all it is, my opinion. You have to make the ultimate choice. Let's start by looking at the facts. Neeka, tell me truthfully, do the girls bristle when you speak?"

Neeka rolled her eyes. "Some do, but they'll soon see I'm just looking out for them."

"Are you sure you're not being too harsh?"

She refused to answer.

"Neeka?" Dr. B prompted.

"Fine. I might be too hard on them. Sometimes," she admitted. "But I just want what's best for everyone."

"No one doubts that," Dr. B said.

Selina smirked, but he turned toward her. "And Selina, is Neeka correct that the team has the potential to play even better than they already are?"

"Of course," Selina said without hesitation. "I was never questioning her motive, just her method."

"Do you remember when we talked about ecosystems? How all life is a result of a balance of forces? Such as when Yellowstone National Park removed the wolf population, which led to an overpopulation of deer and elk?"

"And?" Selina raised her eyebrows.

Dr. B wasn't impressed. "Don't talk to your teacher that way, Miss Cho."

"Sorry," she apologized.

"Like an ecosystem, you need balance on your team. You all have the same goal. You want what's best for the team. You just have different ways of going about it. It's a common hiccup among groups with multiple leaders. The solution is to keep tabs on each other, the way the wolves did for the deer. Selina and Payton, let Neeka know when she needs to pull back and be more supportive. Neeka, you step in when the team is being too lax. Together, you are the perfect volleyball ecosystem."

"Fine," Neeka said, though she was clearly still annoyed.

So was Selina. "I guess," she said.

Payton thought it was a great idea. "Excellent!" she said. "Girls just want to have fun, but we can work hard doing it!"

****

Nashville looked particularly beautiful this afternoon. They drove past Centennial Park, with its lush gardens, lake, and replica of the Parthenon. Payton wondered if she would stay close or go somewhere else for college. It would be hard to leave home. It was a decision she'd have to make sooner than she wanted.

"Do you really think I'm being too harsh on the team?" Neeka asked as she drove.

Payton turned away from the window. "Yes, but not because you're trying to be. I still don't think you fully realize the influence you have over the girls."

"Is it always this hard being a leader? I mean, you've been dealing with this since you were a kid really. How do you do it?"

"I don't really think about it. Back then, I was too young to strategize. The coaches did most of the work. I just yelled out encouragements during the game. You don't think I'm too much like Coach Gina was last year, do you? When she wasn't authoritative enough with the JV girls?"

"If you asked me yesterday, I might have said yes. But our talk with Dr. B helped me put things into perspective. This year isn't the same as JV last year. The girls aren't goofing off. They're just starting to lose their focus. The progress we were making is beginning to plateau, but we can't level off just yet. We're not ready for State. We have to keep going up. It's not an issue of authority. It's an issue of motivation."

Payton sat up straighter in her chair, a thought coming to her. "I'm not so sure it is."

"What do you mean?"

"Selina and I spent the week throwing out encouragements. And you spent the week correcting their mistakes. But there was no improvement."

"That's because we weren't on the same page."

"No, I think it's because the girls know what they need to fix, and they have the motivation to do so, but now we need to show them how. The girls aren't losing focus. They just don't know how to improve."

"I just assumed they would take the corrections I gave them this week and go home and practice."

"But sometimes practice isn't enough, especially if you're on your own. The girls need individual support. I think Team Scary Pancake need to try to schedule some time outside of practice with each girl alone. Really hone in on their skills."

Neeka liked the idea. "We'll have to get Courtney in on it. She's by far the best hitter on the team. She can even help you, me, and Selina improve our skills."

Payton looked down at the folder on her lap. "Speaking of skills, I wish I could add more to my resume."

"It wasn't because of our lack of experience that the zoo never called," Neeka said sympathetically. "They just didn't have any positions available. Who knew there was already a waiting list just to work there?"

"So where is this mystery place you want us to apply for? It worries me that you're keeping it a secret. Is it the garbage dump?"

Neeka laughed. "No way! Trust me, you'll like it. I saw an ad in the paper this morning. I couldn't believe it."

Eventually, Neeka parked near the planetarium. In front of the dome building, giant models of Jupiter, Saturn, and Mars sat on the grassy front lawn. The concrete steps leading up to the building had black glittering stars traced onto them.

"What do you think? They're currently accepting applications."

Payton was amazed. "It's perfect. Let's just hope they call!"

CHAPTER 13

The gym in the fitness center was more crowded than usual. With basketball season approaching, a lot of b-ball players were trying to get a bit of practice in. To accommodate everyone, Dorothy had created a sign-up chart by the hour. Payton waited patiently on the floor by the sidelines for her time slot to begin, watching a group of young girls as one of their moms taught them how to dribble.

She couldn't remember the first time she'd picked up a basketball. Her dad joked that she was shooting hoops before she could walk, but Payton knew he was exaggerating. She had started young, though. She vaguely remembered having a toddler-sized basketball hoop.

She really did love sports. Even if her dad hadn't started coaching her when she was little, she was sure she would have found her way on to a basketball court. It was a part of her. Sports made her happy, more than any other activity she'd tried in her sixteen years.

Even though she'd started out playing volleyball as coordinated as an elephant in high heels, she was glad she'd stuck with it. It'd been the hardest athletic challenge of her life, but that made the new skills she was learning all the more rewarding. She still didn't quite understand why her athleticism didn't translate into volleyball, except that, for some reason, she spent so long worried about what she should do, she forgot to relax and let her instincts take over. But things were different now. She was much more coordinated. Her game had evolved.

"You gonna stare into empty space all day?" a voice asked her.

"What?" Payton asked, looking up to see David standing in front of her.

He held up a volleyball and pointed to the half of the gym that was now empty except for four of the other guys setting up the volleyball net. "Come on, it's our turn."

"You mean it's my turn," Payton said, sitting up from the floor. "I reserved the space to practice my hitting drills."

"Practice on us," David insisted. "I'm sure you'll get a chance to hit at some point."

Payton didn't mind. She preferred it, actually. It was a lot of fun playing with the guys, much more than throwing volleyballs across a net by herself. But she didn't want David to know that. "Fine, but you owe me," she said.

As usual, David took a spot opposite her across the net. "Game on, darlin'."

Today, Payton decided not to hold back. She wanted to dominate, even if it meant taking full control of the court. The guys could save face another day.

"You wake up on the bad side of the bed or something?" David shouted as Payton sent ball after ball his way. "It's raining volleyballs here."

"If you can't take the heat, get out of the kitchen," she said, quoting him from their first meeting.

"At least you're no longer a robot. There's a spark of life in you after all."

Payton couldn't argue with him there. She always enjoyed volleyball, but on the court with these guys, she was able to completely let loose and have fun, like she didn't have a care in the world. And by some magical formula, it helped her play better. She was consistent, getting the ball where she wanted it to go nine times out of 10. But more than that, the more she played with David and his crew, the more she felt that passion that had been missing from her performance, even when David wasn't smart talking her.

And slowly but surely, it was reflecting in her performance with

Hickory Academy as well. When Neeka set the ball or her, she no longer froze up, momentarily thinking about what she was going to do. She just let it happen.

She still didn't hit with the power of Courtney, who by far had turned into the star of the team, surpassing even Neeka, or with the authority of Selina, who could almost tell the ball exactly where she wanted it to go. But Payton was dependable. Her teammates could rely on her to get the job done. That meant more to her than anything.

Her one lingering regret, though she tried to shake it off, was that she wasn't the superstar Annette and the rest of the team thought she'd be when they recruited her onto varsity freshman year because of the athleticism she showed in other sports, like basketball. One of the hopes that had pushed her on over the last two years was that she would eventually reach superstar status, if she continued to improve. She was beginning to realize that, though she was now a strong hitter, she may never be the All-Star in volleyball that she was in other sports.

With this in mind, she couldn't deny that part of the appeal of playing three on three with the guys at the fitness center was because she got a small taste of what it would feel like to be the best volleyball player on the court, of the recognition that came with it.

The fact that I'm dependable more than makes up for not being a superstar, Payton reminded herself. *Being dependable is enough, isn't it?*

****

The next morning at school, Payton hurried toward the lockers just off the East wing. She was running late for her plan. Checking the number she'd written down on the back of her hand, she quickly found the locker she was looking for. She just hoped she'd left plenty of time to spare.

After ten minutes went by and the first warning bell rang, she started to lose hope, but just as she was about to leave, the person she was waiting for came around the corner.

"Well, well, this is quite the turn of events. Payton Moore devoutly waiting for me at my locker," George said with a friendly smile. "Sorry to disappoint you, but the George ship has sailed. You're too late."

"That's too bad," Payton said, "because I was going to set you up with this amazing friend of mine—"

George raised his hand up to stop her. "Say no more. You have my full attention. As long as it's not Selina. I'm not into all that heavy eyeliner and make-up."

The idea of Selina and George together was so comical, Payton almost burst out laughing, but she held her tongue.

"The problem is, George, that if I told you, this girl would literally kill me, especially if you don't like her back."

George looked intrigued. "Wait, this person already likes me? I just assumed you were taking pity on me for all my failed romantic gestures last year by setting me up on a blind date or something. Who is she?"

"Again," Payton said hesitantly, "she would kill me. So I'm not actually going to tell you."

George frowned. "If this is a game, I don't get how to play…"

"I'm going to help you figure it out. But promise me, George, when you do, you have to swear you won't go blabbing it all over the school. If you don't like her back, that's fine, but don't be too obvious about it."

"Payton, I'm not that kind of guy," George said seriously. "I respect girls, especially those who have great taste in men." He smiled.

"Okay, so this girl is a friend of mine. You know her. And you'll be able to tell she likes you because she'll be acting totally different around you."

George's smile grew bigger. "So are you essentially giving me permission to chat up all your friends? This is my lucky day!" He rubbed his hands together. "Who to start with…"

This interested Payton. "Actually, that's a good question. Of all my friends, who would you start with?"

"If I told you, that would ruin the fun, wouldn't it?" He winked.

"Please never wink at me again," Payton said.

The final warning bell rang.

George gently set her aside so he could reach into his locker. "Let the games begin!"

****

"There's a rumor going around that George is chatting up every girl on the volleyball team," Neeka said with despair as she sat next to Payton at their table for AP Biology.

Oops, Payton thought. Maybe her plan wasn't such a great one after all. What if George started to like another volleyball player? She quickly scanned her brain for a way to solve the problem, but she couldn't think of anything.

"I wonder where he is. Class is about to start." She looked toward the front of the room at Rose, who had an empty seat next to her.

"I hope one of the girls slapped him in the face and he's at the nurse's office," Neeka grumbled.

Dr. B started the class by introducing them to the concept of homeostasis, where a cell stabilized its internal function even when outside conditions were changing. Even though she didn't understand half of the words he was throwing at them, Payton internalized the topic, reminding herself that no matter the outside pressure when it came to volleyball, such as other teams believing they had paid their way through the championship, she had to continue working hard and growing. Dr. B finished his lecture and moved on to the experiment they would be performing: taking each other's heart rates in various conditions of stress and relaxation, then graphing the results.

Still, no George.

Payton was starting to worry. It wasn't like George to miss class. To disrupt class with his antics, yes. But not to miss it completely.

Neeka was equally worried. "George did come to school today, didn't he?"

Payton could hardly tell her about the conversation she'd had with George that morning, so she instead answered, "Yeah, I saw him around."

"Well, it's not a family emergency. Rose is here."

Knowing there was nothing they could do, as they took out their graph paper, they moved on to job talk.

"Maybe it's for the best we haven't heard anything back from anyone," Payton said. "It meant we were free during the volleyball season. It would have been difficult juggling a job with all the extra practices we've put in."

"I suppose," Neeka said, dejected. "But I have to start working soon, even if it's only on the weekends."

Seeing how troubled Neeka looked, Payton finally gave in to a thought she had long been pushing away. "Why don't we go ahead and apply for the smoothie place? I was joking before, but it makes sense, really. If we end up working different shifts, I won't need a ride. I can just walk down after school."

Neeka looked equally displeased by the idea, but she resigned as well. "It might be our only option. Let's give them our resumes this weekend."

As Dr. B began his next demonstration, George suddenly burst into the room.

"I'm here!" he announced, taking his place next to Rose.

Dr. B did not seem at all pleased by the interruption. "Mr. Biggleton, we will discuss your tardiness after class."

Payton watched as Rose mouthed, "You're so embarrassing" to her cousin.

George didn't seem to mind the reprimand at all. He stared gleefully toward the front of the room, a twinkle in his eye.

I hope he hasn't gone and asked out someone else, Payton thought. *Neeka really will kill me.*

****

When class was over, Payton hung back, telling Neeka she'd catch up to her. She wanted to discuss something with Dr. B. She just hoped whatever reprimand he was going to give George, it was quick.

Payton stood next to the man in question as the other students filtered out of the room.

"You look happy," she commented.

George swung back and forth on his tip-toes. "I am, thanks to you."

Oh no, Payton thought. "Why is that?"

"You'll see."

Super oh no. She knew George hadn't spoken to Neeka all day, which meant whoever had put this smile on his face—it wasn't who Payton intended.

Before she could probe further, Dr. B called George over to his desk. "Could you please give us a minute?" he asked Payton and indicated toward the door, his way of asking her to step outside.

"I don't mind if she stays," George said. "Let me have it!"

Dr. B folded his hands. "I try to treat you students like the young adults you are, but more than your unexcused tardiness, I can't have you flaunting the fact you were late by disrupting the class. I'm sorry, but I'll have to give you detention."

Payton was shocked. She'd never seen Dr. B give anyone detention before. Then again, she'd never seen anyone announce their tardiness as blatantly as George had before.

George didn't seem at all upset. In fact, he ate it up. "I understand. Thank you, Dr. B," he said as he got up.

Thank you? Boy must have eaten his crazy cereal this morning.

"See ya!" George said, hurrying past Payton out the door.

Dr. B turned to her. "Miss Moore, what can I do for you this afternoon?"

"I know your next class will be here soon, so I'll make it quick. I'm really happy at my level of play in volleyball right now, but I can't help but feel guilty that I haven't lived up to my end of the bargain when Annette recruited me. They thought I'd be a superstar. I know my role on the team is useful, but I'm still concerned that I'm not what the team need me to be. I'm afraid I'm still letting them down, especially Coach Mike."

"You did struggle at the beginning, but the past is gone. Now is all that matters." As he spoke, he began to prepare the papers for his next class. "Who do the team need you to be now? A superstar?"

Payton thought about it. "No, I suppose not. That's what Courtney and Neeka are."

"Then who?"

"I guess the just need me to do my best and be a leader."

"And are you fulfilling that role?"

"Yes. I am."

"Then I see no reason why you should feel guilty."

As he finished the sentence, a pair of students walked in, but it didn't matter. Payton had heard everything she needed to. Dr. B was right. Being a leader, keeping the girls motivated, was enough to help her team win. Their undefeated regular season last year and the still good season they were having his year was proof of that.

I've come so far. And I never gave up. In my own way, I am a superstar.

****

After their last class of the day, Neeka followed Payton to her locker. They didn't have practice that afternoon, but keeping up with their new plan, they were going to meet Janette at the community center for some one-on-one training. Payton collected the books she needed for her homework and shoved the others out of sight into the back of her locker.

"Maybe we should call the community center and reserve a space in the gym, in case they're busy," Payton suggested.

Neeka took out her phone to make the call but paused. "That's strange. I have a missed call from an unknown number. Who would call me while I'm at school?"

She pressed the phone to her ear to listen to the voicemail. As she did, her face went from confusion to absolute excitement. Without speaking, she tugged at Payton's arm and held up the phone, putting it on speaker.

"... highly impressed with your dedication to cosmology and would like to schedule an interview with you regarding your potential future working at the planetarium..."

Payton covered her mouth to keep from squealing. The planetarium! That was a dream come true for Neeka. There was no better job for her. Not for the first time, Payton was suddenly irritated at the fact that her mom had yet to live up to her promise to give her a phone when she turned sixteen.

"Until you start driving, I see no reason why you need one," her mom had said.

But what if the planetarium had called her too!?

When the message was over, Neeka stuffed her phone into her pocket and jumped up and down. "We might be working at the planetarium! Is your mom home? Call her and see if they left a message for you too!"

"No point. I'll be home before mom is. This is so exciting!" Payton exclaimed. "And don't worry, if I haven't received a call, I won't be mad."

"Thank you," Neeka said, placing a hand on Payton's shoulder.

"You two seem happy. You that excited to coach me today?" Janette asked, coming up to them.

"Of course!" Neeka said.

Janette looked regretful. "Oh, I was just joking. I actually found you to say I can't make it today after all. I forgot it's my nana's birthday. The whole family is heading to her house for a BBQ. I'm sorry."

"It's okay," Payton said. "It might actually work out perfectly. It means I can go home and check my messages."

"And I can call the planetarium back," Neeka said.

"The planetarium? That's odd."

Neeka looked confused by Janette's statement. "Not really. My entire life plan is to be an astronaut."

"No, not that. Earlier today, George Biggleton was cornering most of the volleyball players, asking them questions."

"I heard," Neeka said flatly. "Everyone except me."

Payton looked down.

"When he got to me, he mostly just asked what type of activities I was involved in. When I told him I took art class, he then asked if you take them with me."

This clearly upset Neeka. "Why would George want to know if

Payton takes art classes with you? Does he still like her?"

"No, not Payton. You, Neeka. He wanted to know if you take art classes with me."

"Why?" she asked, her voice squeaking.

Janette shrugged. "He didn't say. But then Selina joined the conversation. Overhearing what he'd just asked, she told him you didn't have time for art classes because you were too busy finding a job. He asked where and she told him you and Payton both hoped to work at the planetarium."

Payton was shocked. "That can't be a coincidence. But I don't understand the connection." She looked at Neeka, who had no response.

"Really?" Janette asked. "I haven't lived in Nashville long, but even I know the Biggletons own a lot of property around the city; nearly every educational attraction you can think of, they have some connection to. I'm not sure George has the authority to hire you, but he would certainly have enough sway to push your application to the top of the list."

Payton was flabbergasted. Parts of this situation made so much sense, but some parts made no sense at all. Surely George couldn't have figured out so quickly that Neeka was the friend who liked him.

"George is in detention. Maybe we should go ask him if he had anything to do with the phone call."

Neeka was troubled. "I can't. I'm too embarrassed."

Janette swung her backpack over her shoulder. "I have to go, but I'll say this. I'm not sure if he's still hung up on you, Payton, and he's trying to finally win you over by pulling a favor in for your bestie, or if he now has his eye on Neeka, but one thing is for certain, he certainly likes one of you." With that, Janette left them alone.

"Janette read my mind," Neeka said. "He's obviously still in love with you."

"I wouldn't be so sure about that," Payton said. "Listen, stay here a minute. I'll be right back."

"What! Why?!"

"Just trust me."

Praying Neeka stayed put, Payton quickly made her way to the detention room. She found George at the back, headphones in his ear as he read through his history book.

He looked up at her when she tapped him on the shoulder. "What? You locked up for breaking hearts?"

"Not funny," she said, sitting in the desk next to him. She quickly looked at the clock. They had a few minutes before detention officially started and the no talking rule was in place.

"Did you put a word into the planetarium?"

He smiled sheepishly. "I may have made a call at the start of AP Biology saying a couple of Hickory Academy students had sent in job applications. Now that my voice sounds a little older, it's really easy to sound like my dad when I need to."

Payton laughed. "You are impossible, George. But I'm confused. I only talked to you this morning."

"I already knew Neeka liked me," George admitted. "She's been acting strange around me since the start of the school year. And I've been thinking about her too. But I didn't want to tell her I liked her, in case there was any chance it would cause a divide in your friendship. I know how important you are to her. But after you essentially confirmed my suspicions and gave me your blessing this morning, I decided to go for it."

Payton shook her head, amazed. "Neeka is one lucky girl, George Biggleton."

"Well, you know me, I like my big gestures."

"And do you have any other big gestures in mind?" Payton probed.

"There may be one or two giant gold star-shaped balloons in her locker right now. You'd be amazed how easy the combinations are to break. You just have to listen for a click—"

Payton stopped him. "I do not want to be an accomplice to any future crimes you may commit." She smiled. "I guess I'll be seeing a lot more of you around."

"I hope so," he answered.

Before the teacher in charge could mistake her for one of the detentionees, if that was a word, Payton quickly left the classroom, thankful to find Neeka still standing where she left her.

"Please don't tell me you went and talked to George," Neeka pleaded.

"Never mind all that. I think you should go have a look inside your locker, jelly bean. And after, I know a guy who could use a little company in detention."

CHAPTER 14

Neeka watched as Val taped another volleyball to the wall of the grand hallway of their school. For every victory Hickory Academy earned, a volleyball had been created out of thick white cardboard paper, and the name of the school they'd conquered written in blue marker on the top with an X through it. Every volleyball that went on the wall was a moment of pride. It gave them confidence, and kept them going as they pushed themselves through their team practices and their individual practices. It was nearing the end of the regular season, so there were a lot of volleyballs on the wall.

But the one Val was putting up now was different. The girls felt a special pride at the big blue X on it.

Written underneath the X was Demonbreun High.

All the girls in the volleyball program, JV and varsity alike, had ceremoniously gathered round to watch Val tape it up, cheering as she did.

"Kind of feels like we're putting heads on spears, like they did in the old days to ward off their enemies," Selina mused.

"That is totally disgusting," Courtney said next to her, looking ill at the thought of Selina's comment.

"But it is a warning, in a way," Payton said. "We'll be playing Demonbreun at the District Tournament in less than two weeks. And we're going to win!"

"We will if we continue to practice the way we have," Neeka corrected, not wanting the team to get off track.

They had lost their undefeated title to Demonbreun High, but they were still the number one seed in the district, with their arch rivals following closely behind. Neeka contributed a lot of their success to the fact that Team Scary Pancake, with Courtney's help, had practiced individually with most of the girls on varsity, and she knew each girl was taking the training to heart, practicing during their free time whenever they could, sometimes even at lunch.

It had sparked a fever in them. They had the heat and were ready to take on whoever came their way. Neeka was relieved they'd all worked so hard. It had been easier to keep her inner Annette in rein. With Payton and Selina to balance their leadership out, the team was doing well. But still...

It's easy to gloat when you're the best in the district, Neeka thought. *I just hope the girls don't lose their confidence when we hit Regionals.*

Payton nudged her slightly. "You got that grandma look about you again. Relax, Neeka. We're on top of it. Enjoy it."

"I'm not sure I can relax, not until the season is over," she confessed. "I'm not sure any of us should."

The next day, Neeka picked up Payton from her fourth driver's license test. In the back of her jeep, she had a dozen balloons waiting and a giant card with a dancing hot dog. One the card, she'd written: *License or no license, you're still fantastic.*

Payton's grim expression as she jumped into the passenger seat revealed all.

"You'll get it next time," Neeka reassured her.

"Maybe I wasn't meant to drive. Maybe you're meant to be my chauffer forever. I kind of like that idea."

"And I kind of like the idea of you walking right now," Neeka teased.

Payton looked into the side mirror and spotted the balloons. "Those for me?" she asked, becoming more upbeat.

"Consolation balloons. There's a card too. I'll give it to you later, when we get home."

"Why, where are we headed now?"

"To the planetarium. We're picking up our uniforms, remember?"

Payton buckled her seatbelt excitedly. "I'd totally forgot. This is great! I'm so glad we finally got a job. And that we get to work together!"

"Yeah, George is an angel," Neeka said, blushing slightly.

Payton considered this. "Maybe more like an angel with horns. He also has a devilish side."

Neeka couldn't dispute it. It was one of the things she liked best about him. They'd spent all of detention passing notes. The teacher in charge had never questioned the fact that she was there, nor had he really paid any attention. In fact, she was pretty sure the teacher had been watching a movie on his laptop the whole time.

When they got to the planetarium, Payton jumped out and squealed, "We're here!"

"Remember, we're professionals," Neeka said. "We have to have some composure."

Payton calmed down. "What will we be doing, anyway?"

"Gift shop."

Payton rolled her eyes. "That's a far leap from the zoo."

"Hey, it's better than making smoothies. Plus, we get free passes to a lot of educational hot spots around the city, like the science center and a few of the museums."

"Do they count the fair as an educational hot spot? Free tickets would be great!"

"Doubtful," Neeka said.

They entered the building. The planetarium was privately owned. It didn't have the same fame as the one connected to the science center, but it was pretty impressive. Before going to the manager's office to collect their uniforms, they stopped in the constellation room. It was nearly pitch black inside, with only a few soft lights on the floor. They had to guide themselves around using hand rails. Sensing motion in the room, the walls and ceiling instantly lit up with what seemed like millions of stars all around them.

"They use voice-recognition technology," Neeka explained to Payton. "You'll learn all about it at our orientation, but I did a bit of research. All you have to do is name a constellation, and they'll launch into the science and mythology behind it."

"That's amazing," Payton said, in true awe. "I bet you could spend hours in here."

"Days, even," Neeka said.

"I know these aren't real stars, but do you think we can still make a wish?"

Neeka looked around her. "We could probably make a million wishes. I'm sure the stars would still hear us."

"Then I wish that we stay besties our entire lives," Payton requested.

Hugging her friend, Neeka replied, "You don't need stars for that."

"Good," Payton said. "Then I also wish we win State."

Neeka bit her lip. "That's the funny thing about wishes. Right now, I'm sure every team in the State is wishing the same thing."

"Then I'll wish a thousand times a day."

With the tournament season starting in a few days, Neeka knew they'd find out soon enough if Payton's wish came true soon.

****

"Deja vu," Payton said as they entered the gymnasium for the District Tournament.

The tournament was being hosted by the Hawks this year. There was a second gym at the nearby middle school, allowing more than one match to be played at the same time. Their district didn't have many teams, and not all the teams had qualified for the District Tournament, but there was still a good number of teams there, including Demonbreun High and the Vikings.

"I get the feeling we've been here before," she added.

Looking sternly at her friend, Neeka reprimanded her. "No jokes today, remember. We have to focus."

Neeka was glad the day of the District Tournament had come. She'd waited anxiously for the start of the tournament season, almost to the point where she just wanted to get it all out of the way. The top two teams at District would go on to Regionals where, likewise, the top two teams at Regionals would go on to the Sub-State Tournament. But Sub-State was a knock-out round. If they lost their Sub-State match, like they had the last two years, their season was over. Knowing the girls were counting on her, Neeka was nervous they wouldn't make it past Sub-State again, not if they suddenly suffered the same mental errors they had during their first match against Demonbreun earlier in the regular season.

"At least we don't have to win today to go to Regionals," Payton said with what sounded like relief in her voice. "We just have to come second."

Neeka shook her head sharply. "That isn't good enough."

"Micro-goals, remember, Neeka. Today, our goal is to make it to Regionals."

"Yes, I know that. But the teams in our district are nowhere near the level the other teams are in other districts. If we can't win District, we can't win State."

Payton nodded, acknowledging Neeka's words.

I hope the other girls are focused on winning and not merely slipping by in second place, Neeka wondered.

As the team warmed up for their first match, Neeka observed her teammates carefully. They chatted away happily while they stretched. Courtney told them a volleyball horror story about her team back in California. They had gone swimming the night before a big championship match, but whoever was tending to the swimming pool put too much chlorine in the water. It turned all their nails and hair blue, especially the blonde girls, which there were a lot of in California thanks to the sun. They had to play the championship match the next day looking like icicles.

Her story was funny, but it was not what Neeka wanted. The girls should be talking strategy, not hair. They needed to concentrate.

Neeka stepped forward, wanting to put to rest any fears she had that they weren't in total game mode. "The grand hallway at home is covered in the names of the teams we defeated this season, but we might as well tear them all down if we lose at District. It all goes to waste. We're here to win. Focus out there! Keep your eye on the prize. We're warriors! We fight now and celebrate later."

Later, of course, meaning after State.

"Keep it mean, but keep it clean," Courtney echoed.

Neeka saw an immediate change in the girls. They wanted this. Now, they were quiet. Now, they each wore a serious expression. Now, they were in game mode.

That's it, ladies, Neeka thought. *Just like you're going to war.*

****

Neeka kept on top of the girls for the entire tournament. She didn't want them to become too lax, especially as they started winning, taking an early lead in the competition.

"More momentum, Courtney. Keep the kill shots coming."

"Don't get tired now, Val! Dig deep!"

"Payton, pace yourself. You're moving too fast. It's affecting your accuracy."

"Use those legs, Selina. Jump higher."

At this last comment, Selina glared at her and said, "Why the evil cheerleader act?"

"It's called being supportive," Neeka answered.

"Then how about a little less disapproval in this so called 'support' you're dishing out?" Selina snapped. "Ever hear of something called encouragement?"

"Fine. I encourage you to use those legs to jump higher!"

By the time the girls played the last semi-final match, they were exhausted. Neeka could see it in their faces. They wanted to win so badly. They were really throwing themselves into every second of every play. Recognizing this, it came as no surprise to the crowd in the bleachers when they won and moved on to the final.

"That means we're definitely going to Regionals!" Payton cheered. Taking on a deep robot voice and swinging her arms, she added, "Micro-goal, accomplished."

Neeka shot her a warning look but said nothing.

Coach Mike called a team meeting before the final. He gathered them around under one of the basketball hoops while the tournament took a slight recess to prepare.

"As expected, we're playing Demonbreun High in the final. You've done an excellent job in this tournament. I don't think I've ever seen you play so well. I know you've been practicing a lot, and it's paying off."

"Thanks—" Courtney began to say, but he raised a hand to stop her.

"But I don't want you to lose focus. Stay loose, keep your eye on the prize. Listen to my instructions. Got it?"

"Got it!" the girls shouted.

"Good, now let's leave Demonbreun High begging for mercy."

"Right!" they shouted.

Neeka had been hoping he'd say more. He usually gave such passionate speeches. Feeling there was more to say, after Coach Mike left to attend a meeting for the coaches, Neeka dived into her second speech of the day.

"We let Demonbreun beat us once. We haven't let them do it again. Today is no exception. This is a test. How well we do against our rivals is a sign of how well we'll do at Regionals, Sub-State, and ultimately, State. I don't just want to win. I want us to destroy them," she said.

"Rip their teeth out!" Selina added.

"Ewe," Courtney said, examining her nails. Then, as a side note, she added, "I can't wait until I can have my gels put back on. Having short nails is the only thing I don't like about volleyball."

"Courtney!" Neeka and Selina scolded.

She didn't flinch. "All right, Scream Team, I'm focused. Chill."

"You better be," Selina said. "For once, I agree with Miss Bossy Pants here." She indicated toward Neeka. "We have to make a statement so that everyone at Regionals knows exactly who they're dealing with."

On the court, with the entire district watching, Hickory Academy did just that. They made a statement. Demonbreun High didn't stand a chance. No matter how well they fought, this time, it wasn't enough to keep Hickory Academy at bay. The girls in blue and green were simply too strong for the girls in yellow and black. It was an easy victory.

Neeka watched with satisfaction as the redhead of the team glared at her, her face full of disappointment.

****

"We creamed them!" Payton exclaimed in the locker room after the final.

But she was the only one excited by their large win. The rest of the girls were extremely subdued, barely speaking, although they had smiles on their faces. Neeka assumed it was because they were all tired. Tournaments were tough. They required multiple matches to be played in one day. And today, Hickory Academy had played hard.

"Why is everyone so quiet? This is really freaking me out," Payton whispered to Neeka. "It's like that scary movie where no one can talk."

Neeka couldn't help but laugh. Payton really cracked her up sometimes. "We're just tired. And we're staying grounded. It's a good thing. We have Regionals next."

Payton wasn't convinced. "Come on. We just slaughtered Demonbreun High. We should be hitting our heads on the ceiling like Mexican jumping beans."

"We can't underestimate the teams we'll face in the Regional Tournament," Neeka insisted. "We can be Mexican jumping beans when the season is over."

"We're a lot stronger than we were last year," Selina said, joining the conversation.

"Yes, but we only got to this point because of the extra practices we put in. We need to keep going strong with those practices. That way, everyone stays sharp. We don't have much time between now, Regionals, and Sub-State."

"I hate agreeing with you, Leigh, but our practices before Regionals were kind of light last season," Selina admitted.

"We couldn't have won State those years, even if we had crammed practices in at the last minute," Payton said. "Our skills hadn't developed yet. We weren't good enough."

"But this year, I think we are," Neeka claimed. "We can go all the way, if we maintain our focus. That's why I think we should ask Coach Mike to be extra tough on us."

Payton didn't look as though she liked the idea. "He's pretty tough as it is."

"Don't you want to end the season knowing we did all that we could?"

"I guess..." Payton said, thinking it over. "Okay, I'm in."

"Me too," Selina said.

They took their idea to the rest of the girls who also agreed.

"It's what we need," Val confirmed. "Coach Mike can't allow us any let downs in practice. That's how we'll win State."

****

Coach Mike gave them what they wanted. Practices following the District Tournament were tougher than ever. According to him, he was giving them the "college-level" treatment. Their drills were more advanced, involving complicated rotations that kept Neeka on her toes. She never had to work so hard to prove herself in volleyball. She was glad. It was a good feeling, knowing she was making progress, improving to the point where she could carry the team to State.

Along with Coach Mike being extra tough on them, the rest of the players stayed on each other as well. In some ways, the arduous practices were even more productive than camp. The girls were really pushing, not wanting to let each other down. It proved a better motivational tool than trying to contradict the girls at camp who claimed they had bought their way into the championship.

By the end of the week, they were rock solid. She could see the intensity in the girls. There was no more joking around or chatter. They were totally focused and full of confidence. For the first time since joining the volleyball team, Neeka really felt they had a presence, the same type Jackson Central had, the type that only came knowing you were a superior team.

But Coach Mike didn't seem so certain that the change was for the best.

During the middle of a hitting drill, he blew his whistle for them to stop and pay attention. "Who are you girls!" he yelled. "I've never seen you so stone-cold."

At first, it was hard to tell if he was criticizing them or praising them.

"It's a good thing, right?" Neeka asked.

"No!" he barked.

Neeka immediately slunk her shoulders. *Harsh*, she thought. She didn't understand. Coach Mike was always telling them to stay focused. He had agreed to be strict with them. Why was he unhappy that they were doing so well? Weren't they giving him everything he had ever demanded of them?

"Listen," Coach Mike began. "I agreed to push your skills. I never thought that by doing so I would be pushing the fire right out of you. Who's having fun?"

All the girls raised their hands.

"I mean, as much as they used to."

Only Selina raised her hand. "Knowing we're going to dominate at State is fun!"

Coach Mike didn't look pleased. "Well, you ain't going to win anything playing as tense as you are. When you get under those big glossy gymnasium lights, surrounded by lots of fans and teams that are more experience than you are, you're going to tense up even more. You'll be tight. That's nearly as bad as being unfocused."

Absorbing his words, Neeka wanted to protest, but something inside made her pause—the part of her that knew he was right.

She suddenly felt bad, worried she had taken the fun out of volleyball for her team. She thought back to the story Jamari had told her last year about the coach he had that was so focused on winning, no one was having any fun. She also thought back to Coach Hopkins at camp. *Volleyball requires heart*, she'd said. *If you stop having fun and lose heart, there's no point playing.*

With the memory, Neeka felt even guiltier, wondering if she had gone overboard once again, but then she shook her head, realizing it was silly. Her team had listened to her because they all wanted to win. And they were stronger because of all their extra practices. She hadn't done anything wrong by asking Coach Mike to be tougher on them. That was the nature of a competitive sport. But what she had failed at was remembering that between working hard, they also had to blow off steam.

Being a leader was way more difficult than she'd thought! Sometimes, it was hard to know what was right and how far she should push. She knew when it came to team unity, she had been a great leader. But the technical side hadn't come as easily for her.

"We do need to blow off steam," Neeka agreed. Payton glanced at her, happy to hear it, but Neeka kept her attention on Coach Mike. "What do you suggest, Coach?"

He thought about it for a minute, then said, "I suggest we give up volleyball entirely. Follow me, girls."

****

Outside on the Hickory Academy playing field, Payton could not stop smiling. Coach Mike had led them out here, as excited about his plan as Payton was. Neeka hadn't been too happy with the whole idea, but Payton's beam was contagious. She felt herself start to relax, despite the green mesh jersey she wore.

"If I knew we'd end up playing flag football, I would have worn my Titans T-shirt to practice," Payton said. "This is a great idea!"

Around them, the rest of the girls were broken up into two teams, facing each other down on the field. Some of them looked just as uncertain as Neeka felt, while others ate it up. The team opposite them, led by Selina, were in blue. Coach Mike stood in the middle, holding up a ball. "The rules of flag football are essentially the same as normal football, but instead of tackling each other, you have to grab the flag attached with Velcro to the bottom of each of your jerseys."

Neeka looked down at the thin purple strip of fabric hanging from her jersey. Football was not her forte. Pretty much anything outside of volleyball was crossed off her list, except basketball. She was certain that purple strip of fabric would be in the palm of the other team's hand before she had a chance to even take her next breath.

"We're here to play for fun. Remember that," Coach Mike said. "If any of you hurt yourselves so close to Regionals, I will personally haunt your dreams."

Then maybe you shouldn't have chosen football to play, Neeka thought, but braced herself as Coach Mike gave Selina's team the ball to begin play.

At first, Neeka took her time moving across the field. It soon became clear who the all-round athletes were. Payton, of course, was a bulldozer. So was Selina and, surprisingly, Janette. Courtney looked queasy at the whole thing, while Val got into beast mode, even though she frequently missed the ball.

Soon, any qualms Neeka had about playing football disappeared. As the girls dodged and ran around each other, she couldn't help but be reminded of the water fights she'd had with Jamari when they were little kids. It was actually a lot of fun.

As she started to get into the game, she felt the weight on her shoulders lifting away. The rest of the team were enjoying themselves as well. Neeka hadn't seen them this relaxed in a long time. For probably the first time since the District Tournament, volleyball was nowhere near their minds.

With the ball in her hand, Janette, in green, slid past Selina, doing a little twirl as she did, like a ballerina, causing Selina to land on her hands and knees. It was a great play. As Janette scored a touchdown, the entire field, including Selina, applauded.

In celebration, Janette broke out into a funky touchdown dance, egging Selina on to join her. Selina did, spinning around like a break dancer. Soon, the entire team was dancing, the ball abandoned on the grass as they figured out who had the craziest moves. Neeka tried to do a wave with both arms. Beside her, Payton stomped on the field like a tribal woman. Val clucked around like a chicken. It was mayhem.

Coach Mike didn't mind at all. "Finally, the sound of laughter," he said, chuckling.

CHAPTER 15

Regionals mirrored the District Tournament in almost every way, including the final, which saw Hickory Academy and Demonbreun meet yet again.

Neeka thought back to what Annette had said about how the Hickory Academy and Demonbreun rivalry meant that the girls challenged each other, kept them pushing to be their best, and that Demonbreun was one of their greatest assets.

She supposed it was true. Demonbreun was better than ever. Neeka knew a lot of that had to do with Hickory Academy doing so well. They were using Hickory Academy as their measuring stick. They wanted to be the dominant team once again.

It could likely happen, one day. Neeka knew that. But it wasn't going to happen this year. The final was over before it began. She could sense that the girls on the other side knew they couldn't beat Hickory Academy, but they still fought hard, pushing both Hickory Academy and themselves to their limit.

When Demonbreun lost, their season wasn't over. For coming second, they were still going to Sub-State. But they'd have to play away, while Hickory Academy, having won, would get the home court advantage. But the odds of Demonbreun and Hickory Academy meeting again this year was very low. For now, as they shook hands after the Regional final, they all recognized it was the last time they'd likely play each other until next season.

Knowing such, the air between them suddenly changed. It became much friendlier, almost turning to comradeship.

"Who would have guessed two small schools from our district would be heading into Sub-State together," the Demonbreun redhead said to Neeka as they shook hands. "One of us needs to win State. I don't think any team from our district ever has. We have to cheer each other on."

Neeka was touched. "Let us know when your Sub-State match is. If our matches don't overlap, I'll make sure the Hickory Academy girls are there to support you."

The redhead smiled. "That'd be great."

The celebrations for Hickory Academy didn't stop at winning the final. In the closing ceremonies of the Regional Tournament, Courtney was announced as MVP, which she earned for having the most kill shots.

Selina was disappointed, but she didn't hold a grudge. Not outwardly, at least.

Despite all the celebrations, Neeka still felt a weight on her shoulders. They were heading to Sub-State now—the farthest Hickory Academy had ever gone. In the last two years, they'd failed to make it past Sub-State. Neeka wanted that to change. She wholeheartedly wanted to leave behind the ultimate legacy when she graduated—a State trophy. So though she was happy they were going to Sub-State again, she wouldn't be fully satisfied until they were at State.

****

"Do you think Jamari will make it down for State?" Payton asked Neeka's parents while they all enjoyed a post-Regionals family dinner.

Neeka immediately looked up from her penne pasta. "Payton, please, we have to focus on Sub-State first. We can't go into Sub-State overconfident. It's a sure sign we'll lose."

"But we're so good this year. We could easily beat Cumberland Lake if we were matched against them."

"Possibly, but there are stronger teams out there than Cumberland Lake. Look at Jackson Central. And Templeton. And Bridgewater. And those are only the teams we met at camp."

Payton scrunched her nose, but said nothing.

After Regionals, she, her parents, Mr. Moore, and Payton had chosen to eat at a nice Italian restaurant near where Regionals had been held. Mr. Moore had read a good review of it, so they thought they'd take the opportunity, since they were in the area. Neeka felt as if she was sitting in a castle. The walls around them were made of grey stone, and the place was lit in candlelight. Reproductions of Renaissance paintings such as the Mona Lisa hung on the wall.

"When do you two begin work at the planetarium?" Mr. Moore asked.

"They're going to let us start after the volleyball season is over," Payton answered.

"And what about the basketball season? You're going to be captain of the varsity team this year. What about your obligations to the basketball team?"

Payton's face went red. "I don't need to work as hard at basketball as I do volleyball. I'll be fine."

"I just don't understand why your mother insists you work. You learn enough responsibility through team sports."

Neeka tensed and snuck a look at her ma. Lawanda Leigh did not look happy.

Her ma cleared her throat. "I, for one, think Allison has made an excellent parental decision. It's good for the girls to work, to learn the value of a dollar," she said.

Clearly not wanting a heated discussion to break out, Payton stabbed her chorizo with her fork and held it up. "Do you know what I call a chorizo?"

"The Italian hot dog," they all answered simultaneously and broke out into laughter.

Everyone except Neeka. She couldn't get State out of her mind. She knew she was obsessing, a bad habit of hers, but she couldn't help it. It meant a lot to her teammates. And to her.

Her father reached across the table and set his hand over hers.

"What's stressing you, pumpkin?"

"State," she admitted. "This will be our third year going to Sub-State. We've seen how good other teams are once we reach the Sub-State level. I'm afraid our nerves will make us tight." Neeka suddenly thought of Payton's hot dog joke and turned to her friend. "Payton, you're a comedian. A terrible one, but a comedian nonetheless. You have to help me and the team stay loose, just like Coach Mike said. If we tighten up, it's the same as being unfocused. You're used to this type of pressure."

"As the worst on the team or as an All-Star basketball player?" Payton asked, fiddling with her fork.

"Both," Neeka admitted.

Payton didn't look too confident. "What if I need you to keep me loose?"

"We'll help each other. Agreed?" Neeka asked.

Payton looked up at the Mona Lisa painting and smiled. "Agreed."

****

"I'm panicking!" Neeka said to Payton as the girls lined up at the bench in the Hickory Academy gymnasium for their Sub-State match.

"Already?" Payton asked. "We're not even on the court yet."

"No, not that! I mean, yes, that. I'm nervous about the match. Murfreesboro Valley are total unknowns. They've made it this far, so they must be awesome. But are they more awesome than we are or less awesome remains to be—"

Payton grabbed her by the shoulders. "Neeka, calm down. What has you panicked?"

Neeka took a deep breath to steady herself. She couldn't believe it. What would her ma say? She was going to be in so much trouble...

"Neeka?" Payton prompted.

"George is here."

Payton laughed. "Really? That's what's got you all crazy-eyed?"

"I haven't told my parents yet that I'm dating someone."

Payton's eyes went wide and she squealed. "So you and George are officially dating?!"

Oh yeah, I haven't told her. With all the pep work they'd done for the tournament season, Neeka had completely forgotten to tell Payton the George update.

"Its early days. We've been texting ever since I spent detention with him. We haven't officially been on a date yet. I've been too busy with school and volleyball, but he's started to refer to me as his girlfriend."

Payton was speechless. She just grinned at Neeka with a huge smile that nearly burst her cheeks.

"Stop it!" Neeka laughed. "You look like one of those scarily cute cartoon characters."

"I still don't understand why you're so panicked."

Neeka looked at her blankly. "Really? It's George!"

Understanding, Payton nodded. "Got it. The king of romantic gestures." She looked around. "But I don't see any oversized balloons or banners professing his love. He's not dressed up in any weird costumes. In fact, he's simply walking—"

She stopped, and her face went pale.

"What?" Neeka asked, afraid to turn around and look at the bleachers behind her.

"Don't look," Payton warned.

Which, of course, made Neeka turn around immediately. To her horror, George was walking directly toward her parents.

"I think I'm going to be sick," Neeka said.

"Do you want me to see if I can knock him out with a volleyball? I have a few seconds..."

But it was too late. George sat directly next to her papa and shook his hand, obviously introducing himself. Next he shook her ma's hand, and then Jamari's. Sitting on the other side of Jamari, Brandon and Allison Moore greeted George with a polite wave.

"I am so un-boyfriending him," Neeka screeched.

"I think it's kind of nice," Payton said.

Neeka turned to her friend, a wicked smile in her eyes. "Really? Well, I wonder if David is going to introduce himself to your parents."

Slowly, following where Neeka was pointing, Payton looked up to where David Span, the guy she'd been playing three on three volleyball with, was sitting.

"I'm going to kill you," Payton seethed between her teeth. "He'll scare the young children around him."

Neeka laughed. "Just returning the favor."

"You're cruel. You know he's too old for me."

Briefly, Neeka was afraid she'd made a mistake. But then she remembered how well Payton played at the fitness center. "I actually didn't invite him to set you guys up. He's here because he's your magic bean, remember? You play so well when he's around."

"That's because he's usually throwing banter my way. I'll never hear him from way up there."

"Just pretend. Imagine it. Remember everything he's ever said to you."

Neeka watched as Payton's fists clenched.

"That a girl. Get fired up."

Jamari suddenly appeared by their side. Neeka swore he had been a ninja in a past life. "How you feeling, sis?" he asked.

She suddenly felt an overwhelming gratitude that her brother was there. He'd flown all the way in to be here for her. He said it was perfect timing; his school had recessed so they could study for their mid-term exams. But Neeka knew he would have come anyway.

"Nervous," she admitted. "I'm trying to relax, but it's hard."

"Then I probably shouldn't tell you some guy just introduced himself to Ma and Papa and asked their permission to take you out on a date."

"He did what!"

Jamari held his hands up, grinning with amusement. "Chill. Ma was really impressed. She said he was a good Southern boy for having such manners."

This actually did help Neeka relax. "She was okay with it?"

"Yeah."

"Thank God."

"I guess that counts as a big gesture," Payton said.

"Huge," Neeka agreed.

The Murfreesboro Valley girls suddenly called out a loud chant, grabbing the attention of everyone in the gymnasium and causing their fans to wave around their purple and white banners.

"You think you can beat them?" Jamari asked.

"We've watched a few videos. They're hard to read. They have excellent servers, but so do we. To prepare, all week we've practiced digging the ball and making our passes more accurate. So we'll see."

The officials took their seats at the table.

"Looks like you're about to start," Jamari said. "I'd better take my seat."

He turned to leave, but Neeka called his name.

"Yeah?"

"Thanks, Jamari. And I miss you."

"You too, sis," he said, then pushed his way through the crowded bleachers to rejoin their family, waving at her as he took his seat.

"Let's do this for him," Payton said.

Neeka nodded. "Yes, let's."

* * * * * * * * * * * * * * * * * *

Winning the coin toss, Murfreesboro Valley started the game with a jump serve. Val dug it out, but only barely. She lost control of the ball as it made contact against her arms, and it went flying out of bounds.

A very early and very easy first point went to Murfreesboro Valley.

Their second serve stayed in play a lot longer. The ball reached Neeka, who set it for Selina. Using her arms for mass momentum, Selina struck it with full power over the net, but it was partially blocked, bouncing off the side of the middle blocker's hand.

It stayed in play, and when Hickory Academy returned the ball, the Murfreesboro Valley *libero* passed it to their setter, preparing to attack. When the ball came spiraling over, Neeka watched in fear as it passed through the gap between Payton and Courtney's hands.

"Close that block up!" Coach Mike shouted from the sidelines.

But Val got to the ball, and a true rally took place. Neeka's confidence began to build. It still wasn't clear who the stronger team was, but Murfreesboro Valley wasn't going to crush them, not the way Cumberland Lake had the previous year. That knowledge alone was a relief.

The match turned out to be a long one. It moved at a slug's pace. Both teams were perfectly astute, but they were also equally matched in their speed and accuracy. It meant long rallies that felt as though they never ended. When one team did score, the other wasn't far behind.

Janette loved it. Worried the starters would tire before the match finished, Coach Mike made frequent substitutions, putting Janette in almost as much as Neeka.

"Make every move count!" Neeka shouted from the bench during one of her breaks.

By the time they reached the fifth set, the match was well over the usual time it took for a team to win. But the Murfreesboro Valley and Hickory Academy fans were loyal. They stayed in their seats, cheering on every point scored.

Neeka looked into the crowd. Keeping good on their promise, Demonbreun High was front and center, half their faces painted black, the other half blue. Hickory Academy had gone to their Sub-State match the day before. Sadly, they'd lost. It was now up to Hickory Academy to lead the district to victory.

I never thought I'd be sad at a Demonbreun loss, Neeka thought.

Now that they were in the fifth set, they only had to play to fifteen points. For every set before, the match point was twenty-five, but the winning point had to be by more than two above the other team, so nearly all the sets had gone over. In the longest set Neeka could remember ever playing, the score for the second set totaled 37-36 before Murfreesboro Valley earned the two point lead they needed to win. But by tradition, the match point for the fifth and final set was fifteen.

By the time the score reached 10-10, Neeka was starting to feel the fatigue. She knew they all were, but it worried her. She didn't want Hickory Academy to lose its spark.

Her turn to serve, she put as much energy as she could into her jump serve, but her muscles wouldn't obey. The serve was easily blocked by Murfreesboro Valley. Selina and Payton both crashed to the floor to recover it, but they couldn't.

The point went to Murfreesboro Valley.

It was now 11-10.

Neeka slapped her hands in disgust. This was exactly where Hickory Academy was before—they always got so close but then it all slipped away.

Knowing the match point was close, the crowd jumped to its feet. From the bleachers, Neeka heard Hickory Academy fans cheering for them to get the ball back. Simultaneously, the Murfreesboro Valley fans were screaming for their team to end it now.

Neeka wouldn't let that happen.

"Imagine that State trophy in our display case!" she shouted to her teammates. "Make it epic!"

This seemed to revive the girls slightly, enough that Hickory Academy won the serve back after another long, tough rally that left her bones aching for a rest.

11-11.

During their quick huddle, Neeka focused on Payton, whose turn it was to serve. "I think you're still our secret weapon, Payton. We're all playing at full capacity, but I think you still have a bit of something in you—that fire. When you serve, just picture that it's David's face, okay? Imagine he's heckling you with that big ole volleyball face of his."

This caused Payton to burst out laughing so uncontrollably, she could barely walk to her position behind the back line of the court. Though they didn't know what was happening, watching Payton almost wet herself with laughter caused the other girls on the team to break into giggles.

"What's going on out there? Look mean!" Coach Mike shouted.

This only made Payton laugh harder, but as the ref blew his whistle for her to serve, she immediately focused, turning serious.

Her serve had so much power in it, Murfreesboro Valley only barely managed to recover it. A short rally followed, ending when Courtney fooled the Murfreesboro Valley blockers and dinked the ball over.

11-12.

Between Payton's power serve and Courtney's clever point, the Hickory Academy girls came back to life. They only needed three more points to win, if they could catch a two point lead.

Before the next serve, Courtney turned to the players on the bench. "Come on, now!" she yelled.

Their JV and varsity teammates stood up in their seats at the bench and cheered, which put the crowd in the bleachers in a tizzy.

"Be ready!" Neeka warned her teammates. "Because they're going to be ready."

Payton's next serve was an ace. The Murfreesboro Valley *libero* didn't have a chance to touch it, and it landed in the back corner.

11-13.

It was the two point lead they needed.

Immediately, the Murfreesboro Valley coach called a timeout.

As the Hickory Academy girls grouped around Coach Mike, he pointed at Payton. "They called a timeout to throw you out of your rhythm, Moore. Don't lose it."

Payton didn't seem to hear him. She was agitated, having already figured out why Murfreesboro Valley called a timeout. Shuffling from one foot to another, she looked like a caged tiger. Neeka had never seen her so angry.

"Payton?" Neeka called, but Coach Mike stopped her.

"Let her stay in the zone. This is good."

Payton's next serve was brutal. Murfreesboro Valley had a hard time passing it. It was too close to the net by the time the setter tracked it, making it impossible for her to set it up for an attack. Selina saw it as an opportunity to stuff the ball, earning Hickory Academy another point.

11-14.

From the stands, a familiar chant rose from the crowd.

"One Moore Minute!"

"One Moore Minute!"

"One Moore Minute!"

The end of the match came quick. With fire boiling out of her, Payton scored with an ace. As the ball hit the floor, Neeka did too, but it wasn't purely out of exhaustion.

Hickory Academy was going to State.

Someone slapped her on the back. When she looked up, Courtney stood nearby, screaming her head off, her cornrows shaking around in an almost magic spiral of motion. Then Neeka was picked up off the floor and squished into a gigantic team hug. Somehow, in the mass of bodies, she found Payton.

"I told you to picture David's head!" she said joyfully.

Payton tackled her into a hug within the hug and laughed.

Soon, the Demonbreun High girls and their families joined them on the floor. Neeka managed to make her way to the bench, where Coach Mike had their Sub-State championship T-shirts waiting. Taking one, Neeka stood on a chair and held it up high.

Everyone still in the bleachers stood, drowning the gymnasium with thunderous applause. The standing ovation lasted for several minutes. Neeka looked toward her family and George on the floor. Jamari caught her eye stuck out his tongue. Then he gave her a big grin.

This is for you, she thought.

CHAPTER 16

"This is great, not only are we going to State, but we get to miss school!" Payton stated gleefully as she sat under the willow tree at lunch with Neeka and Selina. "Tuesday equals Tournament Day!"

The State Tournament began tomorrow. Taking place over three days, it meant the entire varsity volleyball team had an excused absence while they were competing. Even better, they'd get to stay in a hotel the entire time! It sure beat the last time Payton missed three days of school, when she had a bad case of the flu.

Selina wasn't as excited. "If I fail History, my parents are going to ground me." She frowned. "I'm doing well in my other classes, but History bores me. It was written by big wigs who want to control how we think about the world. This government did this. This government did that. It makes my head spin. But if I don't show a decent grade on my midterm report card, my parents probably won't let me play basketball."

"Oh no!" Neeka exclaimed. "We'll help you. This weekend, after State, bring all your assignments over to my house. You too, Payton. We'll have a study sleepover. We'll spend the whole weekend catching up."

Payton thought of better ways to spend the weekend. She objected with a joke. "I don't think any of us will be in a *State* to study after this week. Get it. State."

Selina groaned and threw her French fry at her. Having eyed Selina's

French fries all through lunch, she caught it and popped it into her mouth. "Yummy."

"Gross!" Neeka said. "Selina had her germs all over those."

Selina shook her fingers. "All over."

"Will you come, Payton?" Neeka asked. "I really think it's a good idea. I could use a little catch-up session in AP Bio as well. It's a lot harder than I thought it would be! I can't even pronounce half the words Dr. B is making us write down."

"We'll have AP Bio after lunch. Let's talk to the B-man regarding our concerns about missing class then," Payton suggested.

Feeling carefree, she tried to be supportive, but secretly, she thought Neeka and Selina were being a bit ridiculous. They were going to State!!! Who cared about missing class? This was everything they'd worked so hard for.

This isn't the time to cry over homework, Payton thought. *We're about to win State!*

* * * * * * * * * * * * * * * * * * * *

After AP Biology finished, Payton watched as Neeka said a quick goodbye to George, who handed her a bouquet of blue and green colored roses. He wished her good luck, even though he would be traveling down to watch. Not many of their classmates could, but a small caravan was going down the next morning, led by George and Stephen, Val's boyfriend.

So cute.

When George left, the girls approached Dr. B at the demonstration counter.

"Ready for tomorrow?" he asked them as he prepared an experiment for the next class. Something that involved inch worms. Payton shivered.

"Yes and no," she answered. "It wavers."

Neeka took out their syllabus for the semester. "Actually, we were wondering if we could get our assignments ahead of time. With hope, we'll have a chance to do them between matches."

Dr. B clucked his tongue. "Girls," he began, "life is full of many diverse experiences. You'll remember this week at State for a lot longer than any assignments you'll miss during the tournament." He smiled as he spoke, almost giddy.

Marriage sure did change him, Payton thought.

"Concentrate on State. Have fun," he encouraged them. "You can turn your missed assignments in a week after their due date. Does that sound fair?"

"Very," Neeka said.

"Thanks," Payton added. "And not just for this. For everything. You've helped us so much over the past three seasons. You've really been our mentor. We couldn't have gotten this far without your support and guidance. I'd probably still be on JV, having never realized I had such a good jump serve. I hope you know how much you mean to the entire volleyball team."

"Well, I'm profoundly proud of you young ladies. You've both come so far. It's my honor to act as your mentor now and until you graduate next school year. My only remorse is that I won't get to watch you in person play at State. I know how hard you've worked toward it."

"We'll try to bring home the trophy for you and everyone at Hickory Academy," Neeka promised, wiping away a single tear that had fallen.

It is all a bit overwhelming, Payton acknowledged. This was the first time her friend was ever playing in a State Tournament for any sport.

The warning bell for the next class rang. Payton had hardly noticed the classroom behind them begin to fill up with students.

"So many bells, not enough time," Dr. B said faintly. "Congratulations again, girls. And for now, don't worry about those assignments."

****

"Two road trips in one year—I'm liking this," Payton said, settling into her seat in the back of Coach Gina's van.

The school day was over, and they were on their way to State!

Once again, the team was shoved into two vans, but this time, the JV girls who didn't also play for varsity had to stay behind. They were replaced by bags of clothes and equipment. Their luggage was nearly double what they had brought to camp. Being their first time at State, not knowing what they'd need, they'd packed everything they could, nearly their entire bedrooms.

This time, the school was paying for their trip, since it brought them into the media spotlight. Being a school-sponsored event, it meant they would have chaperones. Since all four of their parents had to work, Jamari had volunteered to chaperone Neeka and Payton. He would be driving in his jeep behind the vans, along with the other chaperones, mostly parents, who were coming along.

"Too bad the other JV girls can't ride down with us," Payton uttered.

"I know!" Val exclaimed. "I feel awful. They're part of our sisterhood. They should be allowed. Some will be part of the student caravan that comes down tomorrow morning, but there are a good few who can't risk the unexcused absence."

"I've never been to Knoxville before," Selina said. "But already, it feels like Disneyland."

Neeka, who had been talking on her phone next to her, suddenly piped up. "I have news! That was Jamari on the phone. While waiting for us to leave, he just did some research on the other Sub-State matches. Jackson Central and Cumberland Lake faced each other. Guess who won?"

"Well, Jackson Central beat them last year, so I'm saying it was the same this year," Courtney deduced.

"I reckon that too," Val said.

"That's too easy. Please tell me it was Cumberland Lake," Selina begged. "I'd love a re-match with them. More so than Jackson."

"Why?" Payton asked, honestly curious.

"Because Jackson only beat us in a camp scrimmage. Cumberland Lake stopped us from going to State! I want revenge."

It was scary how matter-of-fact Selina was regarding payback.

"Well, that may just happen because Cumberland Lake did win," Neeka revealed.

"Yes!" Selina threw her fist into the air.

"Calm down. We don't know if we'll play them or not."

Selina was barely listening. She rubbed her hands together. "I'd love to beat them in the final. It would be sweet, glorious revenge."

"Still," said Neeka, "It would have been great to play Jackson. We'd really be able to see how far we've come."

Payton raised her hand. "I think the fact that it's a Monday afternoon and we're driving to State says it all."

CHAPTER 17

The first thing Payton noticed about their hotel was the fountain with a sculpture of a woman on a horse in the front. She wondered who it was supposed to represent. Maybe Calamity Jane or another female hero from the Wild West. Though, she wasn't quite sure Knoxville was wild. Or even in the west. She wasn't sure. She fell asleep during the drive.

As they entered the hotel lobby, the second thing Payton noticed was Lacey Knox checking in.

"Lacey!" Neeka screamed beside her.

Hearing her name, the blonde-haired, blue-eyed, half-Latina girl smiled, and the girls went running up to her. Payton thought she heard Coach Mike yell something, but she didn't pause to listen. She could hardly contain herself. She'd missed Lacey a lot.

Lacey had been a setter on the Hickory Academy team, along with Neeka, until her graduation last school year. More than that, she'd been a really good friend, the only person on varsity not to snub Payton her freshman year when it became clear she wasn't going to be the volleyball All-Star they had hoped. Lacey had made the experience almost bearable.

"It's Lacey Knoxville!" Payton joked, giving her a hug.

"We didn't know you were coming," Neeka cried.

"Well, I was trying to surprise y'all. So... Surprise!"

At that minute, Jamari came in hauling both Payton and Neeka's bags.

"If you think I'm going to be your caddy while I'm here, you're mistaken," he grumbled beneath the mountain of bags. "I'm your chaperone. That means you have to work for me."

Dropping the bags to the floor, he instantly saw who they were talking to. "Lacey," he said, doing a double take. "You're here already. I didn't think you were coming until tomorrow morning."

"I changed my mind." She beamed.

"Wait," Neeka said. "You knew Lacey was coming? How?"

Jamari was at a loss for words, but less embarrassed, Lacey spoke up. "Our schools are only an hour's drive from each other. Being so far away from home, it's nice to see a familiar face, so we've met up a few times."

Payton raised her eyebrows. *It's Team Jacey! Just as I predicted!*

"In what way?" Neeka demanded, her arms folded.

Instead of answering, Jamari instantly grabbed his sister by the shoulder and guided her away, back toward the entrance. "Coach Mike wants you all to meet him by the fountain. While the chaperones check you in, he's going to take you for a tour of the stadium you'll be playing in."

Stadium—not gymnasium. Wow.

"But—" Neeka protested, but Payton took her hand.

"We'll see more of Lacey later. Right now, I want to see the stadium."

As Jamari had said, their team was lined up around the fountain waiting for them.

"Nice of you two to finally join us," Coach Mike said.

"Lacey Knox is here," Neeka explained.

It was clear from Coach Mike's eyes they were instantly forgiven. Lacey had been well liked at Hickory Academy, by students and teachers alike.

"It took us a little longer than expected to get here. Visiting hours at the stadium are closing soon. I want to take you gals down there so you can get your bearings. You've seen large gymnasiums before, but this will be the first time you've ever played in a stadium."

"All my dreams are coming true," Selina said wistfully.

They jumped back into the vans and drove a short distance to a giant arena. They could see it in the distance before they arrived. It stood out against the skyline, like a great big welcoming side that read: *You made it to State!*

The inside was just as impressive. The ceiling looked as high as the sky itself. It was endless. Massive stadium seating surrounded the floor from all four sides. The floor itself currently contained two volleyball courts, with press boxes stationed in front of each court.

Payton had played in stadiums before in basketball, but she had never played volleyball in one. She was glad they had played in large gymnasiums beforehand, like the old gym at camp. Otherwise, she'd be afraid this would have been too overwhelming for her teammates.

"Oh my stars," Neeka breathed next to her.

"Will there be two games happening at the same time? Right next to each other?" Courtney asked, indicating the two volleyball courts.

"Prior to the semi-finals, yes, you'll be playing side by side with another match," Coach Gina said. "But the semi-finals and the final will be a single match."

"With everyone's eyes on us," Val said in awe.

"You can't let it throw you off," Payton told them. "None of this matters. The only thing that matters is the court."

"Precisely," Coach Mike said. "Get your shock out now, because when we come back tomorrow, I want your only focus to be on the game. No excuses. You're the underdogs again. The other teams here expect you to lose. Process that now and spit it back out. Never forget who you are or where you came from. You are Regional Champions three years in a row. Your hearts beat blue and green. Own it. Make State yours. And remember, audiences love an underdog. Remind them why."

****

In their hotel, Payton shared a room with Neeka, Selina, and Janette. There were two double beds that they'd paired up in. She and Neeka had tried to grab the one closest to the window, but Selina had beat them to it. Between the four of them, it was nearly impossible to see what other furniture was in the room. Everything was covered in equipment and luggage.

"Please try not to drool on me during the night," Neeka said to her as she put lotion on her legs.

"Well, try not to snore in my ear," Payton shot back. "When we went camping over the summer, I think the campsite next to us was seriously afraid there was a bear roaming the woods."

Neeka stuck out her tongue. "That was my papa snoring, not me."

Selina and Janette, who were already in bed, Janette with giant curlers in her hair, burst out laughing.

"If you two are going to bicker all night like a couple of nanas, I'm demanding another room," Selina teased.

They ignored her.

"I can't believe how big the stadium is," Neeka said. "We won't know where anyone is sitting."

"Exactly how many of our classmates are coming up?" Janette asked. "I know a few JV girls are joining the caravan tomorrow morning, but I wonder how many more are going to risk the unexcused absence. I mean, it is three days, if we make it to the final."

"We will," Payton said confidently. "We're going all the way! I just know it."

They had improved so much. Payton was so proud of herself and the girls. She really wanted to bring home the State trophy, not just for the glory of the win, but as final proof that when you didn't quit, if you worked hard, like she had, anything was possible.

"It probably won't be many," Neeka warned. "But the tournament is televised, so a lot of the students will be cheering us on from home. I think some of the teachers are even going to show our matches during class."

"That's pretty awesome," Janette said. "Even without our classmates there, I'm excited to see what the atmosphere in the stadium is like."

"It's going to be mental," Payton promised.

****

At breakfast in the hotel dining area the next morning, Neeka pushed her food around her plate. She wasn't very hungry. Her nerves were setting in. Their first match that afternoon would be the first time in the history of the Hickory Academy volleyball program that they played at State.

"Worried?" Payton asked, reading her face. She also had barely eaten the eggs in front of her, which was a rare occasion for her friend.

"Yeah, the significance of this has hit me," she confessed. "This is Hickory Academy's first ever State match. We're writing history. I just hope it's a happy ending."

"I know," Payton said. "It's easy to talk about how we're going to win State, but now that we're here and so close to actually doing it, I'm more nervous than I am excited."

"Maybe we put too much pressure on ourselves. Maybe for this year, it should be enough that we're just here," Neeka suggested.

"It is enough. It has always been enough. But that's not going to stop us from wanting to win."

Neeka knew Payton was right. They had to try to focus while also remaining relaxed, so that they weren't too tense or timid on the court, but that would be very difficult to do with the State trophy hanging over their heads.

Her phone suddenly beeped.

It was a message from George. Or, more accurately, a photo. In it, a good handful of cars were lined up down the street in front of the smoothie place near their school. Each car had blue and green ribbons tied to it. Students stuck their heads out of the windows and sun roofs of the cars, their faces painted in the same color as the ribbons.

The caption of the photo read: The Caravan of Hickory Academy Love.

Neeka smiled and showed the photo to Payton. "Looks like the caravan is on its way."

****

That afternoon, as Hickory Academy took their places on the bench to warm up for their first match, a small section nearby cheered loudly. Neeka looked up to see her family sitting among the caravan of students, glad the troop of Hickory Academy fans had scored seats nearby. Almost all held up massive banners in their hands.

I bet they can see those banners in space, Neeka mused.

The stadium was a quarter full, which was more people than Neeka thought would be there. A quarter was impressive. Next to them, the second court on the floor was also preparing for a match. She knew there was a risk her team would be distracted by the other match next to them, but she was pretty sure they'd be okay. They had learned to shut out everything around them over the last few years.

Just beyond the corner of their court, a colossal video camera was set up. Neeka assumed it was the type they used in movies. Knowing her school was watching them on TV, she stood up straighter, wanting to make Hickory Academy proud.

But no matter how straight she stood, it couldn't stop her nerves eating away at her. This was immense—the stadium, the knowledge they were competing at State, the television coverage. They were most definitely the underdogs here, the less experienced team. They had no idea what to expect. It was completely uncharted territory for them. She tried to block the thought out, but it kept finding its way back in.

She wasn't the only one who was nervous. The entire team was. As they took their positions on the court, Payton tried to loosen them up by telling a groan-worthy joke, but it didn't help.

Payton tried again. "How do prison inmates contact each other?"

No one answered.

"On their cell phone."

Neeka cracked a weak smile, but it was no use. She could feel her muscles tighten, and her mind continued to wander.

Get yourself together, she told herself. *You cannot blow State on the first match.*

However, after the match began and Hickory Academy, within what seemed like a blink of an eye, lost four easy points to their competition, that was exactly what Neeka was afraid would happen. They had barely started play, and Hickory Academy was already sinking, going down fast.

Coach Mike called an early timeout.

"Already?" Selina asked.

"Sadly, I think we need it," Neeka said.

"But it's only four points," Selina maintained. "We'll find our feet and catch up."

Coach Mike heard her. "I don't want you gals to spend the rest of the match trying to catch up," he insisted. "We're at State, ladies. We've reached our final destination. It's go big or go home. I know you're all nervous. I get that. But this is not some big ole scary stadium. And those are not some big ole scary teams out there. You are the giants here. No one can tread on you, unless you let them. You've worked hard to be here; now you need to believe not only that you want it, but that you can achieve it. Trust in yourself. Don't turn that nervous energy into insecurity. Use it to your advantage. Take control of it and allow it to empower you. Hickory Academy is rough. Hickory Academy is tough. And Hickory Academy has had enough—enough of people doubting us, telling us we're too inexperienced to dominate. Teach everyone here a lesson. Show them what happens when they underestimate the underdog."

Creative Writing at its best, Neeka thought, feeling inspired. It was okay to be nervous. The key, as Coach Mike had said, was to use the energy to her gain, allow it to pump her muscles and give speed to her feet.

After Coach Mike's speech, there was no stopping Hickory Academy. Setting back into their positions, Neeka began to realize playing State was like playing in any other tournament. It was bigger and better—but so were they. They went on to win their first match in four sets.

Their evening match was also a success. The same ease they'd experienced at the District and Regionals followed them into the match. Like them, their opponents were unknown, but it was clear early in the first set that Hickory Academy was the stronger team. They communicated better and were more agile. Winning their evening match put them into the semi-final with the other top eight teams in State.

"In the eight and feeling great!" Payton said as they took their seats near the front row of the stands.

Neeka shook her head, wondering where her friend's energy came from. She was just as excited as Payton that they were doing well, but she was also exhausted after playing two matches that day!

There was one more match scheduled for that evening. Coach Mike thought it was important that they stay and watch it. Hickory Academy would play whoever won in the semi-finals. It would have been an interesting match regardless of who was playing, but to Selina's absolute joy, one of the teams was Cumberland Lake.

"I told you we'd get a rematch against Cumberland Lake," Selina said, plopping down in the seat next to Neeka.

"They have to win first."

"They will."

Like Selina, Neeka hoped they did, as did a majority of the Hickory Academy team. Not for revenge, but for pride. There was no greater pride than beating a team that had once squashed them. It would be the ultimate measuring stick of just how far they'd come, proof they weren't getting ahead on lucky wins, nor that they'd bought their way through the competition. Given that Cumberland Lake had beaten Jackson Central, the teams from camp would know just how talented Hickory Academy, the private school, was.

On her other side, Payton bit into a hot dog.

Neeka gapped at her. Payton hadn't left her side. "How on Earth did you get one of those?" she asked.

Payton smiled, a glob of mustard on her cheek. "I have my ways. Now, if only there was some popcorn. We might be here awhile."

She had nothing to fear. The match was short and sweet. Cumberland Lake won after three sets. Neeka was impressed. The Hickory Academy girls had been cheering for Cumberland Lake the entire match, as quick and easy as it was. But she also knew it spelled trouble for Hickory Academy.

We face Cumberland Lake tomorrow, she thought. *We're a stronger team than we were last year, but it looks like Cumberland Lake might be too...*

CHAPTER 18

"You sure you're not coming?" Neeka asked. She hoped Payton would change her mind. They'd experienced the highs and lows of the last three years together. She wanted her friend there every step of the way, including the last.

To Neeka's disappointment, Payton declined. "No way. I can't go."

"Me either," Val said. "You guys go along. We'll be fine."

Sighing reluctantly, Neeka and the rest of the varsity team tucked themselves into a van and drove to the stadium.

This doesn't feel right without the whole team here, Neeka thought.

Payton, Val, and a few of the other girls had decided to stay behind when Coach Mike announced he would be bringing them down to the stadium to watch the other semi-final matches. All eight teams were playing that day, but Hickory Academy's match wasn't until the afternoon, after lunch. So that she didn't end up overthinking things, Payton had elected to stay behind, and Coach Mike accepted, causing Val and others to follow Payton's lead.

The stadium was more than a quarter full today. Teams that had been knocked out stayed behind to watch the rest of the tournament, enlarging the fan base. Neeka sat next to Coach Mike and Coach Gina, with Selina and Courtney on her other side.

Not long after she settled into her seat, she felt a pair of hands cover her eyes.

"Guess who?" a female voice said.

"Lacey Knox, I would recognize your abnormally large hands anywhere."

As Neeka turned around, Lacey slapped her playfully on the shoulders. "I love my hands," she protested, laughing.

To Neeka's surprise, Annette was standing next to Lacey.

"Hi, Annette," she said.

"Hi," Annette warmly greeted her back.

Hearing them speak, Coach Mike also turned around. "Well, if it isn't the college girls. Sit, sit." He waved his hand down for them to take a seat.

Lacey affectionately played with one of Neeka's spirals. "Annette and I always dreamt of coming to State. We have new goals now, on our college teams, but I'm glad we can experience this here and now with you gals—those we helped train up."

"Technically, didn't Neeka steal your spot on the starting line-up?" Selina asked.

Annette frowned, not used to Selina's mannerisms. They hadn't interacted much the year they had both played volleyball for Hickory Academy.

But Lacey wasn't offended. "Aren't you as smart as ever," she said, tugging lightly on Selina's hair.

Selina smiled.

Neeka appreciated having the girls there. In a way, it was almost poetic. It rounded out their whole experience playing volleyball for Hickory Academy so far, uniting past and present. That was one of the pros of making it so far into the tournament season. When big games approached, all supporters came out to watch, whether in person or on the television.

"When do we play?" Annette asked.

Neeka liked the use of the term *we*.

"After lunch," she informed her.

"Awesome," Annette said and sat back in her seat.

Something about that moment struck a chord in Neeka. She was just so glad the girls, and others, had come all the way here to watch them play, even from out of state. Filled with extra motivation, Neeka felt her toes itch. She wanted to jump down to the court and play Cumberland

Lake immediately.

Lacey and Annette had helped started all of this. There might not be a Hickory Academy volleyball program if it hadn't been for their efforts. Neeka wanted them to be a part of this, whatever the outcome was.

I wanted to beat Cumberland Lake before, but now I want it more than ever.

****

The morning flew by, and before Neeka had time to fully compose herself, their rematch against Cumberland Lake arrived. The winner of the match would only be two games away from a State trophy. As they lined up for their names to be announced, Neeka looked into the stands. The Hickory Academy fan base was about the same—a small handful. But both her and Payton's parents had finally made it down, knowing how important their support was, worthy of taking time off work. Beside them, George and Stephen were trying to start a wave.

When the first name on their team was called, the Hickory Academy fans let out a mighty cheer, their numbers small but their voices loud. The cheer continued until the girls were in their positions, waiting for the ref to blow her whistle, signaling for Cumberland Lake to serve.

"Get ready!" Neeka shouted, just as the ref gave the signal.

The Cumberland Lake server took her time. Dribbling the ball against the ground, she eventually took a few steps back, raised the ball high, and launched a powerful jump serve.

Hickory Academy was ready.

Val was on top of it, passing it over to Neeka who set it for the outside hitters, preparing a clean attack.

Neeka had hoped their defense would have taken Cumberland Lake by surprise, but it didn't. Like a majority of the teams here, Cumberland Lake knew the private school girls could play.

I can't be too upset about that, Neeka thought as Selina sent the ball over the net. It flew past the Cumberland Lake blockers but was recovered in the back row. The ball stayed in play for a few more turns over the net before Cumberland Lake scored the first point.

"Shake it off," Coach Mike said. "On to the next."

Cumberland Lake added several more points to the scoreboard. It was excruciating to watch, but Neeka tried to keep her cool, monitoring the ball as if it were moving in slow motion, like she always had in the past.

Thankfully, it wasn't long before Courtney delivered a pile drive hit, breaking Cumberland Lake's serve and earning Hickory Academy's first point.

"First of many," Neeka said during the quick huddle after. "Let's keep it up."

Cumberland Lake were tough competition. Even though Hickory Academy were prepared for them, it didn't make defending their side against them any easier. It was a hard challenge, one that left Neeka sweating out of her ears.

But we're keeping pace with them. That's the important thing.

Neeka jumped into the air to confuse Cumberland Lake, allowing Courtney to put the ball away.

As they played on, it was hard to tell who the stronger team was. Cumberland Lake was by far more experienced, but as much as they weren't making it easy for Hickory Academy, Hickory Academy wasn't making it easy for them. However, Cumberland Lake took home the first set.

"Way to keep them on their toes," Coach Gina cheered as they met at the bench for the small break before the next set.

"I'd like to crush their toes," Selina said. "All of them."

Neeka patted her on the back, not caring about the sweat that covered it. "It's only fun winning if they're actually physically able to play."

"Perhaps."

Quickly looking up into the stands, a large shiny silver object caught her attention. George had created a star-shaped sign, covered it in foil, and glued block letters onto it that read: *Neeka, You're My Superstar!*

Yep, he was definitely the king of big, romantic gestures.

Unable to contain her smile, she waved up at him.

"Neeka, if you'd mind focusing less on your boyfriend and maybe turn your attention back to what's happening here, in front of you, I'd like to actually coach you," Coach Mike said.

Boyfriend. That was such a funny word to hear with her own name. She had a boyfriend.

"Neeka!"

"Sorry, Coach," she muttered, forcing herself to focus.

"We're going to switch up our rotation a bit. For this set, I want to keep you in the back row as much as possible. That way, we have all three of our hitters in the front row putting pressure on their defense. You can still move forward to set, but if you're coming from the back line, remember not to score."

"Got it," Neeka said.

He turned to the whole team. "Watch their blockers. I notice they have a lot of gaps. Target those gaps," Coach Mike ordered.

His changes were effective. Cumberland Lake were still fierce competition in the second set, but with the changes, Hickory Academy didn't have to use as much of their energy to defend their territory. With the hitters performing at their best, they managed to win the second set.

And then the third.

We're actually going to do this, Neeka thought. *We're going to beat Cumberland Lake.*

She looked at Payton.

"Let's close them out," Payton said. "Now, in the fourth set."

"You betcha," Neeka confirmed.

But the fourth set wasn't as easy. Cumberland Lake regained its strength from the start of the match. The defense on both teams were pushed hard. Courtney and the rest of the hitters worked hard to block each ball, but a lot of the work was put on Val. Both she and the Cumberland Lake *libero*, along with everyone else in the back row, fought tooth and nail. Bodies slammed against the floor to keep the ball in play. Every single player was on their guard.

But in the end, Cumberland Lake pulled ahead and won the set 28-26.

They were all winded after the set. Neeka had never had to play defense as much as she had in this match. She had a whole new respect for Val.

"Push through that wall," Coach Mike said to them. "I know you're feeling that last set. You think you've hit your limit, but push through. Mind over matter, ladies. You have this last set. It's yours!"

Before taking their positions, Neeka gathered the team on the court into a quick huddle.

"This isn't just a matter of advancing on in the State Tournament. This is a matter of pride. Let's give it everything we've got. Get to the ball faster. Jump higher. Serve harder. We're not the only ones feeling the squeeze. We ran them ragged too! So let's send Cumberland Lake home and put them to bed!"

Neeka looked specifically at Payton. "You're still our secret weapon. Remember the match against Murfreesboro Valley? Let's see that jump serve again." She then turned back to the others. "From everyone. Our serve is our best opportunity for attack. I want everyone fired up. Use whatever imagery you have to, but make your serves lethal."

The girls nodded their understanding and broke up into their positions.

Cumberland Lake served first, but the ball went straight into the net, a sign of how tired they were becoming.

A senior on the Hickory Academy team was the first to serve. She blasted the ball over like a hail storm. Under normal circumstances, Cumberland Lake would have been ready, but feeling the fatigue, they struggled to recover it. They were just as tired, but it allowed Hickory Academy time to prepare an attack, earning them their second point of the set.

The senior continued to serve, but eventually her mind could no longer control her matter. The next ball she served was easy for Cumberland Lake to reach, and they took control of the ball.

"That's okay, we'll get it back," Val said confidently from the back row.

A battle of wills ensued. They were all at their breaking point, but neither team wanted to give in. They were fighting to move up in the semi-finals, but they were also fighting for glory. Neither team wanted their extreme efforts, or the bumps and bruises that were starting to form, to go to waste.

Approaching the halfway point of the fifth set, Cumberland Lake managed to take the lead, but only by a small margin.

"Don't lose it now," Neeka said. "We're almost there. Just keep going. We are not going down. Remember what I said about those jump serves."

Two points later on either side, Neeka's turn to serve came. She summoned every amount of strength in her body she could. And she did well, managing to put Hickory Academy back into the lead before her arms, which felt heavy and sore, quit on her, and she accidently served the ball out of bounds.

The teams continued to play neck to neck, all the way to the final three points of the match.

In the end, one of the teams managed to jump ahead, wearing down the other team even more. They used the very last of their strength to take home the game. The match hadn't been longer than average, but it had been one of the most intense games Cumberland Lake and Hickory Academy had ever played.

The final score of the set was 12-15.

The winning team barely had the energy to celebrate, they were so tired.

That team was Hickory Academy.

The final point had been scored by Courtney with one of her super spikes.

Hickory Academy was moving on to the next round of the semi-finals.

Are all our games going to be this exhausting? Neeka wondered as Coach Mike slapped her on the back. First Murfreesboro Valley. Then Cumberland Lake. *I suppose that's the level we're playing at now. It's not necessarily about who is better. A lot of us are pretty much equally matched. It's about who fights the hardest. And the smartest.*

Their parents met them on the floor. They were clearly thrilled. Neeka's papa was bursting with so much joy, she feared he may start radiating rainbows.

"You're gonna win it all!" he said.

"One more game, and you'll be in the State final!" Allison Moore said matter-of-factly, a smile on her face. Neeka had never seen Payton's mom so excited about volleyball, or any other sport, before.

Brandon Moore, on the other hand, was much more reserved than the other parents. "Do you think you can go all the way?" he asked.

Neeka and Payton looked at each other. After playing Cumberland

Lake, their confidence had been shaken. Neeka was starting to think they should change their mindset, to stop pushing for a State win and just be thankful they had come as far as they had.

"We like to think we can," Payton answered. "But..."

Neeka stepped in. "That game was really tough. It was not an easy win by any means. The match really could have gone any way. If the next team we play is better, in any way..."

"You don't think you're quite there yet," Brandon concluded.

The rest of the parents listened quietly, reining in their enthusiasm, though they were still as proud as ever.

Neeka shrugged her shoulders. "We won't know until we play."

****

Bridgewater.

The next team they had to play was Bridgewater. Payton secretly scolded Coach Mike for making them watch the scrimmage of the powerhouses at camp. This was precisely why Payton hated watching other teams play. If the other team appeared better in any way, it was easy to get psyched out.

In their hotel room the morning after the Cumberland Lake match, Payton threw on her jersey, feeling a mix of emotions, from anger to nervousness to hope. Looking in the bathroom mirror, she threw her hair up into a very messy ponytail, hoping the pieces of hair sticking out made her look intimidating. Intimidation might be all they had against Bridgewater.

"You look cray cray," Janette said as Payton stepped out of the bathroom.

"I'm not crazy. I'm mean," she clarified.

Too busy getting ready themselves, the girls let Payton's hair go.

Payton looked around, trying to figure out where her knee pads were. Their room had been messy before, but now it looked like a hurricane had hit. Clothes were scattered everywhere. Janette stood in the corner, trying to match ribbons to her hair. Neeka, who was ready to go, was practicing some setting drills near the door with an invisible ball. Selina had her entire make-up selection spread out over the table. Today, she was putting on dark blue liner instead of her usual black.

A knock sounded on the door. "We meet downstairs in five," Coach Gina said through the wood.

"Where's Jamari?" Selina asked. "Isn't he supposed to be chaperoning? I could use a coffee right now."

"He's not our waiter!" Payton giggled.

"Pus, I think it's us who should be chaperoning him," Neeka huffed. "When he's left on his own, he gets into all sorts of trouble. Once, he thought it'd be a good idea to stick his head between the tiny rails of a museum staircase. Unfortunately, he was in a really boring part of the museum, where they only show old documents. It took hours before anyone found him with his head stuck."

"Sounds like he was a bit of a terror when he was little," Janette remarked.

"Oh, no. He wasn't little. This happened his junior year of high school."

Ten minutes later, the girls were in the vans heading down to the stadium. Payton began to see why the coaches insisted they eat breakfast before they got ready. It gave them time to let their food digest. Already, her gut was starting to feel unsettled with nervousness.

Walking into the stadium, they heard a loud cheer ring out from the stands where their families, friends, and classmates sat. Being the final day of the tournament, their fan base had almost tripled in size.

I guess it's easier to miss one day than it is to miss three, Payton assumed, glad to see more familiar faces had driven to Knoxville to support them. In such an uncertain journey, she considered it a benefit.

Of the Hickory Academy fans, the thing that caught Payton's eye the most was the presence of two inflatable cactuses, a smaller one and a gigantic one that towered above the fans. Little Joe and Big Joe, the school's unofficial mascots. After the girls had taken pictures of Little Joe at camp with them, they had returned him safely to the drama room, but clearly someone else had nabbed him.

Roped across Big Joe's neck was a huge sign that read: *Look where Joe is now!*

Payton didn't even want to know how they managed to convince the stadium security to let them bring Big Joe in, but if she had to guess, the students probably waited to inflate him and his big silly red sunglasses until after they were in their seats.

The television crew was all over Big Joe. They loved him, and so did the stadium crowd, who were pointing and gawking.

The stadium itself was half full. Thousands of people would be watching the match today, and that didn't include the people at home in front of their TVs. It didn't bother Payton. At one of her All-State games in basketball, a national event, she had played in a stadium that had been sold out. But she knew the large crowd would probably have an effect on her teammates, for better or worse.

Coach Mike called a team meeting. His face was completely neutral. He gave no sign away regarding whether or not he thought they could win.

"You know Bridgewater from camp. You're familiar with them. Even I've had coffee with their coach. Use your familiarity with them to your advantage. We know they're a tough team to beat, but every team has weaknesses. I want your bodies strong, but your minds stronger. Outsmart them whenever possible. You got a good night's sleep last night. Use every ounce of that renewed energy to show Bridgewater exactly what private school girls can do."

We don't know Bridgewater that well, Payton thought skeptically. *No one really talked to us at camp, and we never scrimmaged against them.* But she did remember one incident when she'd been knocked to the floor during a drill, and a Bridgewater girl had silently helped her back up.

Is being nice sometimes a weakness? she questioned.

Soon after Coach Mike's speech, the opening ceremonies began, and then it was time to play.

For this match, Payton was going to be a right-side hitter. Taking her position, she messed up her hair even more and tried to send a message through her demeanor that she wouldn't let Bridgewater stand in their way to a State victory.

Hickory Academy served first, but Bridgewater dug it out and sent a kill shot their way. It was a powerful attack that earned them control of the ball.

It was a long while before Hickory Academy got the serve back. When they did, it was Payton's turn to unleash her terror. She didn't need to picture the ball as David's head any longer. Her heart was on fire. Using her famous jump serve, she slammed the ball to the other side. It was an ace.

"Well done!" Coach Mike cheered from the bench.

Payton attempted a repeat performance, but one of the Bridgewater hitters got to the ball, passing it on. The ball stayed in play for a short while before Bridgewater scored.

These girls really were good.

As the match progressed, watching Bridgewater play up close was a lot different from watching them from the bleachers at camp. They were graceful and agile. They had speed and accuracy. And most of all, they were extremely modest. They didn't gloat after they put the ball away. They even offered Hickory Academy friendly smiles from the other side of the net. At one point, when Courtney scored an amazing point for Hickory Academy, sending the ball straight to the floor at lightning speed, the Bridgewater girls even applauded.

This goes against all my instincts, but I actually want to be friends with these girls when it's all over.

Over.

It wasn't a word Payton liked very much, but at some point, everything came to an end. She had assumed the match against Bridgewater would be drawn out, like their previous matches. But it was over before she knew it and she felt as if they'd only been on the court for a matter of seconds.

Funny how fate can be sealed so quickly, she thought.

It had been clear from the start that they were outmatched against Bridgewater. Hickory Academy still pushed hard, never wavering. They scrapped and dived and dug for the ball like their lives depended on it, trying to earn every point they could. But Bridgewater was simply too skilled. They were even better than some college teams Payton had seen play. Bridgewater were lionesses, the leaders of the pride.

When the ref blew her whistle, signaling the end of the match after Bridgewater won their third set in a row, Hickory Academy were disappointed, but they didn't feel remorse for losing. They immediately accepted there was simply nothing more they could have done.

Neeka was right, Payton thought. *Because we worked hard all year, we can't kick ourselves for not taking home the State trophy. All we can feel is pride that we made it far enough to play a team like Bridgewater, that we're nearly equal to such a mighty team.*

Nearly.

As the girls walked off the court, the Hickory Academy fans jumped to their feet, cheering so loudly, for a minute Payton feared they mistakenly thought their school had won.

"Do you hear that?" Coach Mike said, pointing at the fans. "You made your school proud to wave their banner in your honor. You're an inspiration, ladies. And not just for Hickory Academy. This is the farthest anyone in the district has gotten. We still have the consolation match to play tonight, but either way, we're at least fourth in State. You did that. With your hard work. With your determination. With your will power. You may not be taking home the trophy, but you are leaving here heroes."

****

Before the consolation match, Lacey and Annette asked the girls to meet them in the locker room for a private meeting, away from the lights and noise of the arena.

"How are all y'all feeling?" Lacey asked.

Neeka answered. "We set a goal to win State, but we did so as a way of getting as far as we could. I'd be lying if I said we weren't disappointed, but I thought losing would feel a lot worse. Being here, surrounded by the reality of what it means to play State, we're also ecstatic at how well we've done. We may not be number one, yet, but we are one of the top teams. From now on, when we go to camp, everyone will know who we are."

Payton smiled at her friend. Neeka explained how they all were feeling so well.

Lacey nodded in approval. And pride. "The Hickory Academy volleyball program started five season ago, when I was a freshman and Annette was a sophomore. We never could have imagined that, in such a short time, Hickory Academy would be playing for a chance to be third in State. I'm glad you girls recognize the achievement that's been made here."

"We're so proud," Annette added. "Everyone who came before you wishes they could play the game you're about to. I always considered it an honor to have worn the Hickory Academy jersey. But now, I consider it a privilege."

Hearing Lacey and Annette speak fired Payton up, along with the rest of the girls. They carried that spirit with them into the consolation match. Wearing their hearts on their sleeves, they played loose, they played with purpose, they played with passion, and they played to win.

And four sets later, they did win, claiming third place at State.

Hickory Academy would be standing on the podium that night, medals in hand, and a plaque to take home.

Coach Mike was so excited after the match, he scooped up Neeka into his arms and lifted her into the air.

When he put her down, Payton asked her, "Are you okay, jelly bean?"

"Actually, I am," Neeka said. She turned very serious. "I'm so proud of you, Payton Moore."

They hugged for a long time, then Payton pulled away to make sure Neeka truly was okay. Studying her friend, she realized Neeka was merely overwhelmed with all the emotions that came with losing and then winning in such a short time.

"And I'm so proud of you, Renika Leigh," she said, causing them to hug again.

Around them, their teammates celebrated, yelling, "Good game!" and, "We'll party tonight!" It was pure jubilation. Payton wasn't sure they could be happier, even if they had won State.

Selina came up to them, and together, Team Scary Pancake did a massive three-person fist bump, shaking their fingers afterwards like fireworks.

"Boom," Selina said.

Bridgewater went on to win State. At the ceremony that followed, Neeka, Courtney, and Payton received All-State Team accolades, which had the rest of the Hickory Academy girls jumping up and down. Then, with all of them on the podium, Coach Mike was presented with the third place plaque. He immediately handed it to a senior, who, shouting for the others to do the same, ran out onto the floor with it. Recognizing their leadership, the senior then handed the plaque over to Selina, Neeka, and Payton. As they held it up, their team surrounded them to touch it.

Payton, seeing Lacey and Annette near the front row of the stands, momentarily left the huddle to pull them out onto the floor with the rest of the team. The older girls were hugely responsible for the team's existence and success. They should be part of the moment.

Glancing up at her parents, Payton knew they were proud of her. They always were, but this was special. Volleyball hadn't come easy. She could have quit, but instead she decided to improve her talent. And now, here she was.

It wasn't just her parents. Everyone at Hickory Academy was proud of their team. For a large part of the last five years, they'd been the underdogs. But not anymore. Now, they were on top. Ten years down the road, Hickory Academy volleyball players, young and old, would see their third-place plaque in the school's display case and know that the girls who had come before them, those who helped build up the program its first five years, had started the tradition of Hickory Academy going to State.

"Be honest," Payton said with Neeka by her side. "Are you happy with third place?"

"For now," Neeka answered, a knowing smile on her face.

Payton put her arm around her friend and nodded.

There was always senior year..

ABOUT THE AUTHOR

Pam comes from a long line of volleyball lovers, including her four brothers who all played for their college teams and her father who was a coach. Pam has spent the past two years travelling as a physical therapist with a beach volleyball competition circuit. She figures what better way to semi-retire than to travel from one beach to another, watching the sport she loves. In her spare time she is an avid snorkeler and she loves kayaking and walking the beach with her husband of almost 20 years.

CPSIA information can be obtained
at www.ICGtesting.com
Printed in the USA
LVOW04s2303060616

491490LV00029B/922/P